Cupcakes and Corpses Copy

Marcall's Breakfast Cafe Paranormal Cozy Mystery

B I Skinner

Contents

1. Chapter 1   1

2. Chapter 2   8

3. Chapter 3   15

4. Chapter 4   19

5. Chapter 5   23

6. Chapter 6   30

7. Chapter 7   34

8. Chapter 8   38

9. Chapter 9   44

10. Chapter 10   53

11. Chapter 11   63

12. Chapter 12   70

13. Chapter 13   80

14. Chapter 14   91

15. Chapter 15   102

16. Chapter 16   116

17. Chapter 17   123

18.	Chapter 18	128
19.	Chapter 19	132
20.	Chapter 20	143
21.	Chapter 21	150
22.	Chapter 22	154
	Thank You!	158
	Copyright	159

Chapter 1

"Oh yeah? Well, I wish you were dead!" Shauna Davis, the stepdaughter of Morley Haynes, the town mortician, shouts in her stepfather's face before turning on her heel and fleeing the Hotel Glacier. But not before nearly running me over.

The entire ballroom falls silent as her words echo off the tin ceiling tiles. Every head turns to stare at Morley, wondering what all the commotion is about. Morley, red-faced, pivots in the opposite direction, heading back to his seat in the ballroom at the annual Halloween Festival.

The festival is Crested Peaks biggest party of the year. And from the size of the crowd, it looks like nearly every person in town is here, plus the tourists who show up hoping to interact with all the ghosts.

"What the heck was that all about?" I ask as I approach our table.

"I have no idea!" Miranda, my best friend and witching mentor responds. "And I'm guessing I don't even want to know. But nice of you to finally show up."

"I know, I know, sorry I'm late," I apologize as I give my boyfriend Detective Drew Bailey a quick kiss before sitting down. "But I knew if I didn't take the boys trick or treating, I'd never have a moment's peace again."

"I can't even begin to picture how you take two rabbits and a cat trick or treating," Miles, Miranda's boyfriend, says, shaking his head in wonder.

"I put them in the wagon and then we walked around the neighborhood while they begged for treats. You should have seen the look on people's faces when I asked for parsley and bites of chicken.

"I still haven't decided if I should laugh about it or be embarrassed. I'm sure people think I just have overly spoiled pets. It's not like I want to explain to them that my pets are para-pets who can talk and like to demand things."

Miles breaks in. "You could tell them they talk. It's not like people in Crested Peaks aren't aware of all the paranormal activity. Plus, everyone knows that you're a witch."

I nod my head. "I know that a lot of us have familiars, but it's still rather unusual to have familiars that actually talk to their person. And I worry that if too many people knew they talked to me, it would just become a spectacle, and goodness knows I don't need any more of that."

After I came back to Crested Peaks, just over a year ago, to take over Marcall's Breakfast Cafe from my Gran, the two rabbits, their cat friend, and I discovered four bodies. I know how people like to talk in this small mountain town, and I'm not giving them additional fodder.

"If people knew that the rabbits and the cat helped you gather clues, they may not be as open to talking in front of them, right?" Drew points out, his tone dripping with sarcasm. It frustrates him to no end that I always seem to find myself in the middle of solving crimes. I maintain that I can't help it. They seem to just land on my doorstep.

"I told you, I am done with that! No more crime-solving. I'm just a simple cafe owner who's minding her own business. Besides, how many bodies can my para-pets find?"

"I can't believe you just said that out loud!" Damien, my brilliant chef, exclaims. He grabs the salt shaker on the table, shakes some into his hand, curses in Spanish, and tosses it over his left shoulder.

"Superstitious much?" I ask.

He throws his hands up to indicate how we're surrounded by ghosts, wizards, witches, and a whole other host of paranormal beings. Crested Peaks is known for its widespread paranormal activity. Supernaturals and Non Supernaturals live together like anybody else in any other small town.

Right on cue, Harvey, one of Crested Peaks more famous ghosts, appears at our table. "Good evening, my friends!"

"Hi Harvey!" we all exclaim.

"Aside from the ridiculously public display of family discourse we were forced to witness earlier," he whispers, nodding his luminescent head toward Morley, "how is everyone's evening? I take it you're enjoying yourselves on this most festive occasion?"

Harvey managed the Hotel Glacier when it first opened in the late 1800s. It was one of the most opulent hotels of its time. The building materials and fixtures had to be pulled over unyielding mountain terrain using horse-drawn covered wagons. Many of the original designs remain, such as the tin ceiling tiles in the ballroom.

Harvey was killed in a shootout between the sheriff and a bank robber. He claims he was too busy with managing the hotel to bother moving on to the next world for his afterlife, so he just stuck around instead. He's helped me, I mean the Crested Peaks Police Department, solve some crimes. Like the para-pets, people often speak freely in a ghost's presence, because they're assuming they aren't repeating anything.

"Do you happen to know what Morley and his stepdaughter were fighting about Harvey?" Miranda asks.

"I can't say that I'm privy to the details, but she's not the first person I saw him argue with this evening." He grimaces he finds all of this so distasteful. "One would think he could set his issues aside on such a joyous holiday."

I bite my lip to keep from laughing. Halloween is a big deal in Crested Peaks. Especially among the Supernaturals. Don't get me wrong, we just enjoy our holidays in general - any excuse to throw a party - but we pull out all the stops for Halloween.

"Who else was he arguing with this evening?" I ask him right before I take a bite of the fabulous cupcake in front of me. Chloe, our friend from high school, landed a big score when the hotel asked her to provide cupcakes from her food truck, Chloe's Cupcakes.

"Oddly enough," Harvey responds, pointing to the cupcakes in front of us, "it was Miss Chloe herself."

"No way. What happened?" Damien asks as he shovels a second cupcake in his mouth. They're just that good. Chloe is a witch, but her cupcakes recipes are all pure non-magical baking. Although, they're so amazing that I'd swear they really are magical. The decorations, on the other hand, are usually enhanced with some witchcraft.

The cupcakes that Miles brought to the 4th of July picnic had enchanted stars that blinked and shone. Tonight's cupcakes are red velvet, and the decorations include a flying miniature witch, with a black cat riding on the back of her broom that waves at me.

Her red velvet cupcakes are one of my favorite recipes. I'm not entirely sure what the secret ingredient is that makes it so unique. I certainly have my ideas, but I'm keeping them to myself. Whatever it is, it's delicious.

Harvey sighs. "Our disagreeable friend—" at the word disagreeable, Morley just happens to guffaw at a joke someone is telling at his table. He pounds on the table, taking another swig of bourbon. When he tries to light a cigar, one of the wait staff dashes over to remind him he can't smoke inside the hotel.

"As I was saying," Harvey continues to shoot a disgusted look Morley's way, "the mortician couldn't help but goad our lovely Miss Chloe over her new profession. He insisted on reminding her what a horrible beautician she was when she worked for him. He's a most unpleasant fellow all around. I don't know a soul, living or unliving, who likes him."

"Did you know Chloe was a beautician for a mortuary?" Damien's husband, Tom, turns to him in surprise.

"Of course I knew that! You didn't?"

"I never knew there was such a thing in the first place!" Tom exclaims, looking a little green around the gills at the thought.

"Of course there is. How else do you think they make the bodies look so, uh, well, 'natural,'" Damien responds with air quotes.

Harvey keeps going. "Mr. Haynes abused that poor girl to the point she couldn't take it anymore. She quit and took it upon herself to start a business. I daresay she's doing an even better job as a cupcake baker than she did in the mortuary. Not that she didn't do a tremendous job there. I've heard from many of the unliving that they wholeheartedly approved of how she made adjustments to their corpses before being revealed to loved ones."

Miles raises his eyebrows like he can't believe Harvey just said the word "corpses" over dessert.

"In fact, there was one fella whose head was squashed like a cante—"

"Harvey!" Miranda cuts him off.

"I apologize if I've offended anyone's senses, Miss Miranda. I was simply going to point out that when that poor man was crushed by a boulder while hiking—"

"—okay, Harvey, we appreciate your dedication to details, but I don't think Miles can handle your honesty."

"I've overstepped. I would never wish to offend a guest. I'll take my leave now." Harvey says, bowing at us as he drifts away.

"You okay there, big guy?" Miranda teases Miles while patting him on the back.

"I'll live," he whispers, hastily digging into another cupcake.

"I guess Morley is in rare form tonight," Drew points out. "When I came in, he was fighting with Ethan Davis too. Then he shouted 'you're fired'."

"What did Ethan do then?" Miranda asks.

"He ran out the hotel."

"Is there anyone he didn't fight with tonight?" I openly ponder.

"Harvey was right, though," Damien responds. "I don't know anyone who likes him, either. He's a jerk."

Almost as if on cue, Morley stands up at his table. Everyone pauses and stares like they're waiting to see what he'll do next. However, when he clutches his chest, gasping for air, I don't think any of us expect that.

Several people cry out as he pitches forward, grabbing the tablecloth in his meaty fist, sending plates and silverware flying. Then he flings himself backward and collapses, knocking several chairs askew on his way down. The commotion creates near pandemonium in the ballroom as guests cry out in shock and rush toward the table to get a closer look.

"Is there a doctor in the house?" Harvey shouts as he races over everyone's heads to hover over Morley.

Another ghost, who also lives in the hotel, floats over to Morley and hovers for a moment. But lacking the gentlemanly fortitude of Harvey, declares with a shout, "He's dead!"

Drew gasps and quickly dials 911 on his phone anyway to request an ambulance.

Cries of shock and dismay punctuate the previously festive atmosphere of the ballroom, as party goers try to decide if they should move in closer for a better look, or leave as quickly as possible.

I'm horrified when I remember it was just months ago, at another festival, that the rabbits led me to a body. Now we seem to have another one. I'm grateful that this one isn't murder, at least. It's too bad that Morley just died like that. However, I assume from the way he was clutching his chest, and what appears to be an unhealthy lifestyle, he's had a heart attack.

Drew looks at me with dismay, like he can't believe this is happening again, either.

"At least my familiars didn't find the body this time, right?"

Instead of responding, he shakes his head like he can't believe I just said that out loud.

At least Miranda laughs at my inappropriate joke like every best friend should.

"Too soon?" I ask.

Chapter 2

There's a drawback to celebrating late into the evening, especially one that involves a lot of drama. Damien and I are dragging this morning when we arrive at Marcall's at o'dark thirty, as my Gran used to call it.

"Whose idea was it to work in a breakfast cafe?" Damien asks with an enormous yawn as he prepares our coffee.

"Pretty sure you started it." I glare at him through blurry, sleep-deprived eyes.

"But you own the place, so I think you should take responsibility."

Meanwhile, my rabbit familiars, Marshall and Marcus, scurry around at my feet, reminding me how fun trick or treating is for the dozenth time. They want to know if we can do it again tonight.

"Trick or treat is only once a year," I scold them as they pout and stomp their little feet. I'm not sure which is worse. The disagreeable looks they're always giving me or the foot-stomping when they don't get their way.

My grandma always claimed to have won them in a poker game decades ago. Then she named her cafe after them. They don't do magic, thank goodness, or we'd all be in trouble.

But considering your average house rabbit lives about ten years and doesn't talk, we're convinced Gran must have used some kind of magic on them. Either that or they truly came that way, and their previous person only pretended to lose the game, realizing it would be simpler to make them someone else's responsibility.

When Gran was alive, she was the only one they could talk to. But when she passed away, somehow that ability transferred to me. They only weigh about four pounds apiece, but amazingly, they travel all over town begging treats from the shop owners.

"Why are you mad about trick or treating? You hop all over town as it is begging for vegetables and flowers almost every day."

"It was extra fun to go in the wagon last night," Marcus explains, wiggling his crooked ears at me.

"Yeah!" Marshall chimes in. "If you could pull us around in the wagon all the time, we would really appreciate that."

I sigh and look at Damien like I can't believe the plans these two come up with sometimes. "What are they hatching now?" he asks, peering over the countertop at them, looking a little leery. Damien is used to living with Supernaturals, but something about talking rabbits makes him nervous. He was relieved when the rabbits said his dog, whose name is Bubbles, doesn't talk.

"I'm not pulling you around town in the wagon just so it's easier for you to beg treats!" I tell them.

"Fine!" Marshall grumbles as the two of them head back into my office, where Stumpy, the cat, is undoubtedly sleeping. He doesn't appreciate the early cafe hours either.

Their best friend, Stumpy, used to live next door at the Italian restaurant. But after the restaurant owner was stabbed to death, the restaurant's new owner kicked him out. Marcus and Marshall then invited him to live with us. Without asking me, of course.

"Did you forget to unlock the front door again?" Damien asks when we hear someone knocking.

"I did," I groan. I concentrate on the lock, because I'm too tired to walk over there, and it pops open.

"Good morning, everyone!" Gladys calls out to us. Gladys, the provider of our unending supply of town gossip, is here on the dot as usual for her 6:30 AM vegan breakfast burrito and coffee.

I'm almost afraid to go out front and tell her it will be another 30 seconds because we're running just a tiny bit behind.

"Good morning to you, Gladys!" I tell her as I enter the dining area carrying a stack of clean plates.

Her mouth drops open in surprise. "Where's my burrito?" she asks.

"Damien and I are a little slow on the uptake this morning, so it will be—"

"Here it is, Gladys!" Damien announces as he bursts through the kitchen door with her burrito.

Thank goodness, I mumble to myself. I don't know how Gladys would react if she had to wait for more than a moment for her burrito. She schedules her entire day down to the minute, and any unexpected detour from that schedule makes her nervous.

"Party a little too hard last night?" she asks Damien, raising an eyebrow his way.

"It was quite the evening, wasn't it?" he grimaces.

"I'm guessing you have the latest on Morley Haynes?" I prompt.

She snaps her gloves into her matching purse as Damien places the burrito and coffee in front of her. "You know it's odd, but I don't really have anything more than you probably already know, since you were there last night."

"What?" I ask, feigning horror that she doesn't have all the dirt already. Gladys prides herself on her ability to sniff out the latest happenings in our town. And like Harvey at the hotel, and my familiars, she too has helped me, of course I mean the CPPD, solve several crimes.

"Everyone seems extra tight-lipped about Hayne's death. I'm not even getting anything from my sources at the hospital."

"Do they really not know, or are they just not telling you?" I ask as I hand a newcomer our menu for the day.

Gladys slowly shakes her head. "I don't know for sure, I just know that for now, Morley dropped dead at the Halloween Festival and, like everybody else, I'm assuming some kind of heart attack."

After Gladys leaves, the cafe is somewhat quiet all morning. It's the lull before the Crested Peaks Ski Resort opens next week, where we'll be busy with ski traffic and tourists until Memorial Day Weekend.

Thankfully, I hired additional help over the summer. A young woman named Aranya, whose parents own the Thai One On food truck. She's a culinary student at Colorado Mountain College, and has a test this morning, so she won't be in until later.

The customers we do have this morning are abuzz about what happened last night at the hotel. I'm still relieved I didn't stumble across any new bodies myself last night. Considering I was barely back in town a month before I found two of them.

I literally tripped over one and was accused of murdering him. Then Stumpy found a dead mobster in the park, and Marshall and Marcus, never to be outdone, found a murder victim at the 4th of July Festival.

And somehow, I always end up personally involved in the investigations, much to Detective Bailey's chagrin. But I'm done with all of that. I've officially hung up my investigator's hat, and I'm sticking with my vegetarian breakfast cafe apron. Thank you very much. Business is great, and now that ski season is almost upon us, we'll be busier than ever.

During a mid-morning lull, Damien approaches me, looking both excited and nervous. For a moment, I'm terrified he's going to quit because some swanky, high-paying restaurant in Denver offered him a job or something. "Hey boss, I have something to tell you."

I gulp. "Okay."

"Tom and I are applying to become foster parents.""Seriously?" I squeal. "That's amazing! When? Where? How? Oh, my gosh! Can you tell I'm excited?" I'm practically jumping up and down. I'm so happy for them.

"They already have a child in mind for us, but we still have to complete all the paperwork and get approved. I was hoping you'd write a letter of recommendation for us."

"Of course I will! And who's the child? There's so much to do! I'll start writing the letter now!" I exclaim as I head for my office.

"Okay, calm down, Char, not everything has to be done right this second," Damien laughs at me, but I can't tell he's happy I'm so thrilled for him. "She's three years old, and her name is Poppy. Her mom came here from Puerto Rico with her when she was only about a month old. Tragically, a drunk driver killed her mom a couple of weeks ago and they haven't been able to locate any relatives for her yet."

"Oh, that's heartbreaking. And if anybody knows what she's going through, it's me." I was quite a bit older than Poppy when my parents were killed. Even so, I know what it's like to lose someone. Also, my parents were con-artists who were murdered by another criminal in a con job that went awry, but I can still empathize with this poor girl.

"And that's why you'll make the best auntie," Damien tells me.

"I just thought of something. What if they don't find any of her relatives? What happens then?" Thankfully, I had my grandma when I was orphaned. I can't imagine not having anyone, though.

"Wellll," Damien says, tracing a floor tile with his toe and blushing. "It's possible we could adopt her."

I put my hand over my mouth, trying not to cry. "Oh, Damien, that would be the best thing ever."

"Don't get your hopes up!" he warns me. "Ideally, they'll want her reunited with any family she might have, but if that can't happen for some reason, Tom and I are open to adopting her. But let's just take this one step at a time, okay?"

Our low-key celebration is interrupted when Aranya shows up for her shift. "Please don't say anything to anybody else yet. I don't want to tell a bunch of people until we know something for sure," Damien whispers.

I give him a thumbs up and nod my head in agreement.

"Hey, guys! What's up?" Aranya asks, hanging her coat and backpack on the coat rack.

"I was just telling Damien that I think we need another one of Chloe's cupcakes."

"Ohhhhh wow, those things are so good!" Aranya exclaims.

"I could absolutely go for a cupcake," Damien agrees.

I grab my own coat off the coat rack. "It's settled then. Three cupcakes coming up."

"Get some parsley while you're out!" Marshall calls out from my office, where he was supposedly napping.

I roll my eyes at my friends. I can't walk out the door ever without the rabbits requesting some kind of snack. Italian parsley is their favorite, however, so that's their most frequent request. "They're demanding parsley," I explain.

"I brought you something better," Aranya says, digging in her backpack.

That brings the rabbits scurrying out of the office as they watch her pull out two dandelions.

"Awwwww yeah!" Marcus shouts as he leaps into the air and binkys. In case you're wondering what a rabbit binky looks like, it's when they're just so happy they leap into the air and wiggle about. It's quite comical and endearing. But they don't need to act like they're never fed.

"Where did you get dandelions this time of year?" I ask in surprise.

"We're growing them at the school to use in recipes," Aranya explains. "And I know how much these two love them."

She leans over as they each rip one out of her hands. They usually both grab the same one and fight over it, but they must have forgotten that ritual in all the excitement over fresh dandelions in November.

"I won't be gone long," I tell them as I head out into the crisp late autumn air.

Chapter 3

The first snow was about two weeks ago, and we already have about a foot of it on the ground. I relish the crunch of snow beneath my feet as I walk along Main Street, taking in all the Halloween lights the shopkeepers still have out. Pretty soon, the Christmas decorations will replace the orange, black, and purple lights.

Crested Peaks at Christmas always looks like one of those towns you see in a Hallmark Christmas movie, except our snow is real. I notice that snow already coats the mountain peaks and as I approach Chloe's Cupcakes Truck, it's snowing again but lightly.

I stick out my tongue to see if I can catch any, and then I laugh at myself. I can't believe Damien and Tom might adopt a little girl. It will be hard to keep their secret because I'm so happy and excited for them. I hope he at least lets me tell Drew and Miranda. Otherwise, I don't know how I can keep my mouth shut for long.

There's a short line at Chloe's truck. Anywhere else, customers would be scared off by the snow but not in Crested Peaks. We're so used to it here that we just carry on the same as if it were 75 degrees and summer. And because of the ski resort, the more snow, the better.

I line up behind the others, but Chloe sees me and waves. "Hi, Charlotte!"

"Hey there, Chloe!"

"Afternoon snack for everybody?"

"You know it!" Today she's serving hot chocolate, along with the cupcakes. My mouth waters as I watch one of the customers walk away from the truck, clutching the warm cup in their mittens while steam trails from the top when it hits the cold air. I guess I'll make it three cups of hot chocolate in addition to the cupcakes.

I scan the menu on the side of the truck, torn over which cupcake I'll pick today. The red velvet cupcakes from last night were exceptional as always, but now I think the caramel nut fudge sounds good. It's so hard to decide. I may have to get more than one flavor.

I'm so engrossed in daydreaming about delicious cupcakes that I almost miss the fact Drew and an officer have pulled up in a squad car behind Chloe's truck. When I finally see him, I wave at him, but he's so busy talking to the officer with him he doesn't see me.

I'm shocked when they walk around the back of the truck and knock on the door. What on earth? Now I'm worried. Is Chloe in some kind of danger? Is something wrong with the truck? Why are the police knocking on her door?

Chloe looks just as confused as I am when she hears the knock. She holds a finger up to the customer she's waiting on, and he nods as she moves to open the door. When she does, Drew asks her to step outside. I can already tell this isn't a friendly visit. He's acting like it's an official police matter instead. By now, people are gathering on the sidewalk and staring.

"Chloe Miller, you're under arrest for the murder of Morley Haynes," Drew announces.

"What?" I exclaim. He's kidding, right?

Drew finally turns and sees me standing there, my mouth hanging open in shock.

"Charlotte, what are you doing here?" he groans. He's so tired of finding me at crime scenes. And now here I am with ringside seats for an arrest.

I throw my hand in the air. "I'm buying cupcakes. What are *you* doing here? This has to be a mistake!"

"This is official police business. Just go back to Marcall's."

"Don't you boss me around, Detective Bailey!" I even plant myself in Drew's way, which I know I'll hear about later. I know I don't actually have the right to impede police business, but I don't care. "Chloe is my friend, and I demand to know what's going on."

This is preposterous. Chloe would never hurt a person, much less kill them. Even if it was that creep, Morley Haynes. "Morley wasn't murdered, he died of a heart attack. How could that be Chloe's fault?" I remind them.

Drew sighs loudly. A sure sign I'm really in trouble. "Morley didn't die of a heart attack. One of Chloe's cupcakes poisoned him," he whispers so no one else can hear. "Now step back and let us do our job," he growls.

"Charlotte, you have to know I didn't do this. I would never," Chloe begs.

"I know you wouldn't! And I promise you, we'll sort this out," I insist. Drew stands over me, glaring at me with those mesmerizing green eyes of his, and I realize I just put myself in the middle of another investigation. Oops.

At five feet, 10 inches, most people aren't able to stare down at me. But Drew can. And at the moment, he's looking superimposing and all policey. Most of the time, I find this disturbingly attractive. But right now I feel like someone who knows she'll get lectured by her boyfriend later.

He purses his lips at me until I finally step aside, knowing I obviously can't prevent them from leaving. I watch with dismay as they lead Chloe back to the squad car, sliding her into the back seat. Drew doesn't stop glaring at me until he gets in the car himself and drives away.

The crowd gathered around Chloe's truck, murmurs in wonder. News travels fast in this town, and I know it will spread before dinner that Chloe Miller was arrested for murder.

Just as I'm wondering if I should try to close up her truck, the Crime Investigation Unit shows up to search it. I trudge back to Marcall's, wondering how such a great day could go so wrong so quickly and how do I keep getting stuck in the middle of these things?

Chapter 4

I open the door to Marcall's, wondering how I'll tell Damien what just happened. It certainly ruined my day, and I really don't want it to ruin his. But the moment I walk in, I can tell by the looks on his and Aranya's faces they've already heard.

"Unbelievable," I say, slapping my hand to my forehead. "News moves through this town faster than the speed of light."

"So it's true?" Aranya cries out.

Damien points at my hands. "I'd say, given the lack of cupcakes, it is."

Before I can completely shut the door, Miranda bursts in behind me, nearly knocking me over. Not only does news blaze through this town with lightning speed, but without fail, Miranda is always ready to pounce on the revelation. Of course, it helps that she owns the coffee shop across the street Bean Around a Bit, and she keeps an ever-watchful eye on us, lest she misses out on a juicy piece of gossip.

"Holy coffee beans, is it true? Chloe killed Morley? I don't believe it for a second. I mean, she probably hated him enough to kill him, but I know she never would. That guy was such a jerk. But no way she killed him. Did they really drag her from the cupcake truck and arrest her?"

I'm convinced Miranda samples too much of her own product. She's always going a mile a minute. Her spiky hair is still green today, left over from last night's party, where she dressed as Yoda. Which, given her short stature, was perfect. As short as she and Damien are, I swear sometimes I feel like the Jolly Green Giant around here.

"They didn't drag her from the truck," I correct her, shaking my head. Gossip around here gets blown out of proportion just as quickly as it gets passed around in the first place. By the end of the day, they'll be insisting that Chloe engaged in an hours-long standoff with the police, barely escaping with her life.

"You were there?" Miranda exclaims, wide-eyed and shocked.

"I was there. Drew and a CPPD officer pulled up in a squad car, knocked on the door, and asked her to come out," then I hold my hand up to stop Miranda from telling whatever far fetched tale she's about to repeat. "She did so willingly, and then they arrested her. You guys," I continue, looking around at the three of them, "I don't think she even knew why they were there. She was as shocked as the rest of us. Drew said her cupcake poisoned Morley, and that's why he died."

"Whoa," Damien responds. "It wasn't a heart attack then."

"Not according to Drew."

Damien winces. "I bet Drew wasn't happy to see you at the scene."

"Oh, you got that right, my friend. And then when I stood in their way, he was extra unhappy."

Aranya giggles. She giggles a lot, actually. "You stood in their way?"

"It was a spur-of-the-moment thing," I try to explain. "And then I may have told Chloe I'd get to the bottom of all of this."

"No. No, you did not," Damien responds. Damien is often the adult among us. He tries, usually without success, to keep Miranda and me in line. "You can't get involved in another criminal investigation, boss."

"You didn't say that when I was trying to clear your cousin's name a couple of months ago, did you?" Ha! Got him there.

"Okay, I'll give you that one," he responds, his cheeks turning pink. "But you and I both know that Drew will be extremely unhappy if you get involved in this. He hates it when you interfere in police work."

"She's right," Miranda says, stepping up to my side. "No way Chloe killed someone. Not even Morley. Besides, if she goes to prison, who will supply us with delectable cupcakes?"

Damien shakes his head. "You two will use any excuse to get in the middle of an investigation."

"We don't get involved on purpose," I remind him. "These things find us."

"Keep telling yourself that," he mutters, heading back into the kitchen area.

"Several people fought with Morley last night at the party. Not just Chloe. It could have been any of them. Remember, it was his stepdaughter Shauna who said she wished he would die. Right before he actually died," Aranya points out.

"Yes!" Miranda exclaims, giving a little hop, clapping her hands.

"Don't get involved with those two, Aranya!" Damien shouts from the kitchen. "They're trouble!"

"You know we have to talk to Shauna, right?" Miranda asks.

"No, you don't!" Damien insists, poking his head out the service window.

"We so do," I agree. "Does anyone know where she works?"

"She works at the Fly There Travel Agency," Aranya says.

Miranda circles her hand in the air. "To the travel agency!" she shouts.

"Wait!" I urge, grabbing Miranda's arm. "We can't all just go marching in there. We don't even know her. She'll immediately be on the defensive."

"I know her," Aranya says.

"To the travel agency!" Miranda shouts again.

Damien sighs so loudly in the kitchen he sounds like an inflatable raft that's sprung a leak.

Chapter 5

Unfortunately, in our excitement, it doesn't occur to us until we get there that three women storming the travel agency might put Shauna on edge. Especially because I assume she was already stressed out over the death of her stepfather.

Imagine telling a person you wish they were dead and less than an hour later, they are. She must feel horrible. Unless, of course, she's the one who did it.

I didn't even realize travel agencies still existed. I guess some travelers prefer the personal touch of being able to sit in front of an expert discussing their plans and budget, rather than just signing up for a trip and entering their credit card number online.

"Hey, Shauna!" Aranya says as we tiptoe into the quiet travel agency. There's elevator music playing softly in the background, set off by large, squishy-looking furniture. Perfect for relaxing and leafing through brochures and magazines that tell of far-off places.

Shauna smiles briefly at Aranya, but her smile wavers when she sees Miranda and me. "Hey Aranya, what's up?" she asks hesitantly.

"I heard about your stepfather's passing, and I wanted to check in to see how you are doing. And I brought my boss, Charlotte, and our friend Miranda, who owns the coffee shop across the street from Marcall's. We didn't think you should be alone right now."

Not a bad excuse for someone who hasn't done this as many times as Miranda and me.

Shauna scoffs, "I don't care that he's dead. In fact, I'm glad. And I already heard that Chloe, my dad's former employee, poisoned him. Good for her. She should have done it a long time ago. In fact, I wish I would have thought of it."

Not exactly the speech I was expecting. "Er, Chloe was arrested, but we don't know for sure that she did it," I remind her. I bite my tongue to keep from adding that I know it's impossible that Chloe did it because I don't want Shauna to realize that she's a suspect in my mind.

"Whatever," she responds with a shrug. "Morley was a vile person who didn't deserve to live, and we're all better off now that he's gone."

"Shauna, this may be indelicate, but I have to ask, why are you so happy that your stepfather is dead?" I fear that the question may get me thrown out of here, but I really want to know why she's so bitter.

Shauna stands up at her desk, knocking several files to the floor in the process, while Miranda jumps forward to pick them up for her. "You seriously want to know why I'm glad he's dead?" she asks, slamming her hands on the desk.

"Um, yes?" I ponder what I'll do if she leaps over the desk to smack me a good one.

"I'll tell you why. When he and my mother were married, he treated her like crap. I don't know what she ever saw in him or why she even married him. He spent half their marriage drunk and the other half cheating on her without even trying to hide it!"

"I'm so sorry, I didn't realize that," I respond.

"Shauna, I have to ask, why do you think your mother stayed with him?" Miranda adds.

Shauna shakes her head angrily. "He was Mr. Nice Guy while they were dating. Paid all sorts of attention to her, wined and dined her; she was the center of the world. But then he married her and got control of her money. That's when he turned nasty. And everybody warned her about him. Everybody else knew what he was really like, but she couldn't see that in the beginning."

"Did your mom have a lot of money?" Aranya asks. "Because I thought Morley was already extremely well off."

Shauna plops back down onto her desk chair. "There was never enough money with Morley. He always needed more. And my dad's life insurance policy was enough for my mom to pay off the house and not have to worry about the bills. Of course, Morley knew this because she told him all that while making the funeral arrangements for my dad. He knew exactly how to manipulate the newly widowed Mrs. Miller."

"We couldn't help but notice the argument you had with Morley at the Halloween Festival," I point out. We've come this far, we might as well go all the way now.

"I'm pretty sure the entire town saw that," she grumbles.

"Can we ask what it was about?" Miranda says.

"Dear old dad," she responds, her voice dripping with sarcasm, "doesn't approve of my dating Neil Doyle."

"The waiter at the Hotel Glacier?" I turn to Miranda, who nods. "Why does he have a problem with Neil?"

"He's a wizard, and Morley doesn't approve of Supernaturals and Non Supernaturals mixing."

"Oh," is all I can think to say. Except now I'm extra mad. Morley is a jerk.

"Where did you go after you left the hotel?" Miranda asks.

"I came back here to work," Shauna responds. "Neil was working the party, and I needed some space and wanted to cool off. I needed to be anywhere but at the hotel looking at Morley's disgusting, smug face so I came back here."

I have about one hundred other things I want to ask Shauna about her stepfather, but we're interrupted by a couple looking to use the travel agency.

"Hi!" the woman says excitedly. "We need to plan our honeymoon, and we're hoping you can help us."

"Of course, I'd be delighted to help you with that," Shauna says, rapidly switching from someone who was angrily celebrating her stepfather's murder to a professional travel agent in the blink of an eye. "I'll be with you in just a moment."

She turns back to us, "Ladies, I don't know your friend Chloe very well, but I know my stepfather treated her horribly when she worked for him like he did everyone else. And if she really killed him, then good for her, and she shouldn't have to go to jail for killing the devil. But if you're still looking for people who hated Morley enough to kill him, then I'd talk to Ethan Davis.

"Ethan works for your stepdad, right?" Miranda responds.

"And he also fought with Morley at the hotel last night," I remind them.

"Morley used and abused Ethan the entire time they worked together. And I swear he fired him regularly just for sport. Just so he could hear Ethan grovel. If you really don't think Chloe did it, he's one you should talk to."

"Thank you. We appreciate your help," I tell her.

"We'll be on our way then," Aranya says, giving me a look that says we're done here for now.

"Yes, of course, we don't want to keep you from your work," I exclaim. "We're sorry to have bothered you."

"No bother, have a lovely day, ladies," she responds with a huge smile. Wow, that wasn't weird at all.

The three of us file out of the travel agency and turn back to Marcall's. I can only imagine what Drew would say if he realized we seem to have recruited Aranya into our efforts now.

"Now we know what prompted her to shout at him like that in front of everyone at the party last night." Miranda starts off the discussion.

"She doesn't seem to care who knows how much she hated him and wanted him dead, that's for sure," Aranya replies.

"And just when you think Morley couldn't sink any lower, we find out that he doesn't approve of Supernaturals and Non Supernaturals together. He's disgusting." I add.

"This is all really messed up," Aranya says.

"Char, I keep meaning to ask, are you experiencing any psychic energy with this?" Miranda asks.

Aranya stops in the middle of the sidewalk, grabbing my arm. "You're psychic? Why didn't you tell me?"

"It's nothing like that," I explain. "It's just that sometimes I experience these bursts of psychic energy or something. We don't even have a good word to describe it." I shrug. "I don't have them all the time and I can't control them. It usually happens when there's a lot of adrenalin and emotion involved. But to answer your question, Miranda, no, I haven't experienced any of that yet. Not even a whisper."

We file into Marcall's only to find a very annoyed Damien waiting for us. "I can't believe you two have sucked her into this," he chastises.

"We didn't mean to," Miranda reminds him. "But since she actually knows Shauna, she was our best opportunity to get information from her."

"All right then, out with it," he says, passing around sample sizes of his latest dish.

"So, you don't agree with the idea of us investigating who killed Morley, but you're happy to hear about what we've learned?" I ask as I help myself to a bite. With Damien, we never know what new dish he expects us to try next. I pretty much just eat whatever he puts in front of me.

"I agree with Drew. You unnecessarily endanger yourselves when you interfere in CPPD investigations. I worry about you guys, okay, but since you've already done it, you might as well clue me in," he explains as we all gather around a table, snacking on the special oatmeal he's put in front of us.

"This is amazing, by the way. What is it?" Aranya asks.

Damien grins. He loves it when people enjoy his cooking. "It's a savory oatmeal. My grandma always made it. Oatmeal, onion, green pepper, veggie broth, black beans, a bit of cumin, and plantains. A very stick to your ribs kind of breakfast, if you will."

"You want to add this to the menu?" I ask.

"Let me tinker with it a bit," he responds, like always does. If I let him 'tinker with it for a bit,' it will never make the menu, so I'll just add it, anyway. He's such a perfectionist, but that's why the customers keep coming.

We explain Shauna's blatant and loud hatred for her stepdad and how she makes no effort to hide any of it. But we also point out that she left the party after their fight and went back to work, so she wasn't even there when Morley ate the poisoned cupcake.

"But her boyfriend Neil, who Morley disapproved of, is a waiter at the Hotel Glacier who worked that night." Damien says, pointing out something the rest of us missed.

"She told us that," I admit. "And he would have had access to Morley, I assume. And now you're in on it with us!" I tell Damien as I smack him on the arm.

"Don't remind me," he says, shaking his head and getting up to take the empty sampling bowls back into the kitchen to wash, cursing softly in Spanish as I often drive him to do.

Chapter 6

"Now that you two are here and it's quiet, I have something to tell you," Damien announces as he rejoins us in the dining area.

I'm relieved that he's telling Miranda and Aranya, and I won't have to keep this from them any longer. It's such exciting news. It's hard not to mention it every time I think about it.

"Tom and I are applying to become foster parents, and they already have a little girl picked out for us if they approve our application."

"That's amazing!" Miranda squeals. "Wait," she says when she realizes I already knew about it. "You knew?"

"He told me earlier but then swore me to secrecy."

"I can't believe you managed to keep it secret!"

"I assure you, it was painful. Especially news like this."

"Who else knows?" Aranya asks.

"At this moment, outside of my family, just you three. And I would like to keep this as quiet as possible for the time being," he says.

"Is it okay if I tell Miles, though? He won't tell anyone else, and he'll be so happy for you!"

"Yes," Damien relents. "You can tell Miles. And yes, of course," he turns to me as I open my mouth to ask, "you can tell Drew as well."

"Oh, thank goodness," I sigh. "It was killing me to keep a secret this big."

As we all hug Damien and fire questions at him, a customer comes in. "Wow!" he exclaims. "This is quite the party!"

"Welcome to Marcall's!" I tell him. "Where it's always a party!" We all laugh because we're so giddy over Damien's announcement.

"I've heard that your breakfast burritos are the best anywhere," he says. We have a lot of regulars who I know by sight, and many who I even know by name, but I don't recognize this older gentleman at all.

"They are," I tell him. "Thanks to this genius," I announce, patting Damien on the back.

"Well, young man, then get me a burrito, please!"

"Would you like a Damien Special?" I ask. "It's Damien's secret blend of black beans, eggs, cheese, potatoes, grilled jalapenos, and caramelized onions, all layered with a secret sauce."

"That sounds superb. I'll take it!" the man says.

"Coming right up!" Damien proclaims as he hurries into the kitchen to prepare his burrito.

"I don't think I've ever seen you in here?" I ask as I ring up his purchase.

"You're right, this is my first time, and I'm hoping to be amazed."

"I'm sure you will be," I tell him. "And how about a cup of coffee on the house, since you're a first-timer?"

"Young lady, I love this place already."

I pour him a cup of coffee as he selects a seat for himself in the corner. When Damien places his burrito in the service window, I take it and the coffee out to our newest customer. "Enjoy!" I tell him, putting his food, silverware, and a napkin in front of him. "Let me know what you think!"

I return to celebrating with the others, but this time we try to keep it low-key. I promise Damien I'll write a letter of recommendation for him this afternoon and turn it into the foster agency in person. He doesn't think I need to go to that extreme, but I want to know they received it for sure; I don't want to chance it getting lost in the mail or something.

"Excuse me, miss, do you have a newspaper here?" the man calls out to me.

"Yes, we do!" I tell him as I bring him today's paper. I know most people, including me, get their news on the internet, but we have some customers who enjoy reading an actual paper while they eat, so I keep the subscription.

"Hot diggity!" he shouts, smacking the paper where the article about Morley's death sits front and center. "That good for nothing scum bag is dead!"

Uhhhh what?

"Please tell me someone killed him. I hate to think he just died from a simple heart attack. He deserved far worse."

The four of us stare at the man in shock. I don't quite know what to say at this point. Who could have imagined that the death of the town's mortician would engage such passion in so many people?

"I take it you knew him?" I ask.

"Sweetheart, you must be new around here."

"Yes, kind of," I respond.

"Well, trust me. You wouldn't believe me if I told you. I still don't believe it myself."

"Oh," I tell him, hoping he'll expand on his story. Instead, he goes back to eating his burrito and reading the newspaper, so I quietly shuffle off toward the kitchen because I can't think of anything more to say.

I'm dying to ask the others what his story is. From the looks on their faces, I can tell they know, but don't want to say anything in front of him.

"It's been fun, everyone, but I have to get back to my own shop now," Miranda tells us. "Damien, congratulations! I can't wait to hear more when you get approved by the foster agency." Then she makes *call me* gestures with her fingers while pointing her head toward the man in the corner.

Shortly after Miranda leaves, the man brings his plate, silverware, and paper to me at the counter. "Young lady, my compliments to your chef. That was delicious!"

"Thank you so much. I'm glad you enjoyed it. What is your name, by the way?"

"I'm Owen Munoz, and you are?" Owen says, holding out his hand.

"I'm Charlotte. Charlotte Duffin, and I own Marcall's," I tell him, shaking his hand.

"I'm very pleased to make your acquaintance Charlotte, and I'm sure I'll be back to try the other tasty items on your menu."

"I'm looking forward to it!" I tell him as I watch him walk out the door.

But just as the door starts to close, Drew walks in.

Chapter 7

"Drew!" all three of us chorus.

He holds his hands up. "Before any of you can even ask, I'm not at liberty to say a thing about the investigation right now. But I have a free moment, and I wanted to stop in and say hello and get some of your delicious donuts because you know I'm addicted to them. But please, don't ask me any questions."

Last summer, Damien and I developed a donut by combining Damien's cooking talent with a little of my witchcraft. Tastes exactly like a regular donut but with half the calories. We sell out of them constantly and even had a large corporation offer us a ton of money for the recipe. But we'll never tell. We're keeping them in Marcall's, where we have control over how they're produced.

"I hid some donuts this morning just for you, Detective Bailey, just in case."

"You're the man, Damien!" Drew exclaims, pointing at him.

Damien ducks into the back, but not before I notice him blushing. Both he and Tom like to refer to Drew as Detective McHotty behind his back. Yeah, I know, my boyfriend is ridiculously handsome, and sometimes it's downright embarrassing. Even Gladys, who's old enough to be his grandmother, enjoys flirting with him.

While Damien places two donuts in front of Drew, I pour him a cup of coffee. "Since the good detective won't be answering any of my questions at this time, why don't you explain what that was about with Mr. Munoz and Morley."

"Munoz was here?" Drew asks.

"He was leaving just as you were coming in. I'm surprised you didn't see him. And why are you asking like that? Is he a suspect?"

"The better question is, why do *you* ask?" Drew responds. "You know you shouldn't be investigating Morley's murder."

"Because he obviously hated Morley." I throw my hands up and turn to the others. "And I'm dying to know what the story is with him and Morley Haynes."

Damien takes a deep breath. "Owen's wife passed away a couple of years ago over in Cripple Creek where they were on vacation celebrating their 60th anniversary. Morley picked up her body in the company hearse and was supposed to bring her right back here so they could begin the funeral arrangements."

"Uh oh." I already have a bad feeling about where this is going.

Damien nods his head. "Ol' Marley decided to sneak in some gambling at one of the casinos while he was there."

"With Mrs. Munoz body in the hearse?" I ask, horrified.

"Yes ma'am!" Damien confirms.

"This doesn't end well, does it?"

Aranya shakes her head.

"While Marley was in the casino, a couple of teenagers thought it would be funny to steal a hearse and take it for a joyride."

I gasp, throwing my hand over my mouth.

"The teens insisted they didn't mean any harm by it. They just planned to drive around town and take pictures of themselves, assuming they'd have it back in front of the casino well before Morley came out."

"Instead," Aranya takes over, "since they were inexperienced drivers to begin with, they had extra trouble handling a hearse. They hit an icy patch on the road, slid down an embankment, and rolled it."

"Oh, that's awful."

"And it gets worse," Aranya says. "The back door broke open, the casket flew out, and Mrs. Munoz ended up in the river."

"This actually happened. In real life?" This is like a tale out of a movie or a weekly tv crime story.

"In real life," Damien says, nodding his head. "Poor Mrs. Munoz body was then carried down the river. And it just happened to be a year where there was intense water runoff from the mountains, so the river was moving extra fast, which flung her body from rock to rock. By the time she ended up downstream, she was so badly mangled that they couldn't even conduct a showing at the wake.

"They had to cremate her body instead. Owen never blamed the teenagers. He blamed Morley for not coming right back with the body like he promised. Said he couldn't believe that Morley would stop to gamble when he was responsible for something as sacred as someone's body."

"I can't imagine what the Munoz family went through. That's heartbreaking."

"Now you know why Owen Munoz is one of a long string of people who are extra happy to hear of his death."

"Did anybody see Mr. Munoz at the hotel last night?" I ask.

"Oh, no you don't," Drew says. "Just stop right there. I know exactly where you're going with this."

"What?" I ask him innocently.

"You just added Owen Munoz to your list of suspects you want to interrogate, which you shouldn't be doing in the first place."

"I shouldn't be adding him to my list?"

"You shouldn't have a list at all, is my point!"

"I'm just concerned that my friend Chloe, who I know could not have killed anyone, was arrested for murder. If I have ways of finding out things that maybe the CPPD doesn't, shouldn't I assist with that?"

"No!" Damien and Drew say at the same time. Have I ever mentioned how annoying these two can be when they gang up on me?

"Here's what we know so far," Drew says as he first holds up one finger. "Many witnesses saw Chloe arguing loudly with Morley Haynes right before he died. Then he dies after eating a poisoned cupcake." He holds up a second finger. "That poisoned cupcake was one of Chloe's cupcakes."

"But anybody could have slipped poison into that cupcake!" I protest. "Why do you think it was Chloe herself?"

"I already told you, I can't discuss this with you any further. But I swear to you, we are investigating this matter fully, and when I can give you more answers, I will. For now, you'll just have to wait.

"And speaking of work, I have to get back to the station. Damien, thank you for the amazing donuts, as always. And please keep an eye on these ladies for me."

"Aye aye detective!" Damien declares. Ugh. Remind me to fire him soon.

"And you," he says, giving me a quick kiss on the cheek before leaving, "stay out of this investigation. I've got it handled." Double ugh. Remind me to fire him, too.

Chapter 8

At the end of the day, I'm relieved to lock the cafe door and get ready to go home. As if the shock of Morley Haynes dropping dead at the Halloween Festival wasn't enough, watching Chloe get arrested for his murder on top of that has pushed me to the limit. And then hearing about what seems to be a never-ending list of people who wanted Morley dead is exhausting.

I hope the rabbits and Stumpy are in my office where they're supposed to be, so I don't have to drive around town looking for them. But when I peek in the office, they aren't there.

"Does anybody know where the three hooligans are?" I call out.

"Last I heard, they were down at Hotel Glacier hoping to get treats leftover from last night."

"Are you serious?" I ask in dismay. "They had tons of treats last night, anyway. And now I have to chase down there and get them." I jam my arms into my coat, getting more frustrated by the second.

"Okay, I guess I'm headed to the hotel. If they come back, tell them they're to stay put or no carrots for a week."

"Will do boss, see you tomorrow."

I stomp out to my car. I'm so annoyed that sometimes those three are a lot of work. I should just tell them they can get jobs at the hotel and stay there. Although I'm not sure what kind of work they could do other than stealing snacks from hotel guests.

When I pull up to the Hotel Glacier, I see Harvey out front directing guests to the check-in desk. "Good evening Harvey!" I call out.

"Well, good evening to you, Miss Charlotte! Two days in a row. To what do I owe the pleasure?"

"Have you seen Marshall and Marcus and their cat, by any chance?"

"I just saw those rascally creatures a few minutes ago in the lounge, as a matter of fact. I do believe they were trying to talk a young man out of his brussels sprouts."

"Okay, thanks," I grumble as I head into the hotel to collect my erstwhile familiars. But I stop in my tracks when I remember. "Hey, Harvey!"

"Yes, miss, how can I be of assistance?"

"Do you happen to know if an Owen Munoz was at the party last night?"

"Ahhhh, the party where Morley Haynes was thought to have perished from a heart attack but is now considered a murder victim? I assume that's why you're interested?"

"Uhhh, yeah, kind of." I don't want him to blab to others that I've been asking around about the guest list.

"No, I don't believe Mr. Munoz was here last night."

"Oh, okay, thanks." How disappointing.

I make my way back into the lounge searching for Marshall, Marcus, and Stumpy, and sure enough, they're gathered around a busboy, staring up at him with their best sad faces, as they like to call them. They told me this is how they get treats from everyone.

The poor busboy tries to get a full tub of dirty glasses back to the kitchen, but those three are blocking his path. "I'm sorry," he says. "I don't know what you're trying to tell me."

"All right, you three, let him do his job!" I scold them.

Upon seeing me, Marshall and Marcus hop straight at me, with Stumpy hobbling along behind. He gets along remarkably well, considering his back legs are nothing but stumps. He told the rabbits he's an injured war veteran. I'm not sure how that's true, but I'm also not sure how I have talking rabbit familiars either, so who knows.

The three of them bounce around at my feet. "Is it dinnertime already?" Marcus asks.

"Yes, and it's time to go home! What were you doing here?"

"The usual," Marshall tells me.

"All three of you get more than enough food at home. I don't understand why you think you need to beg treats from everyone all over town."

Marcus shrugs his tiny rabbit shoulders. "Because it's fun."

"Whatever, let's go." As the four of us head to the hotel entrance, I remember that Shauna's boyfriend works here and I stop in my tracks. Poor Stumpy isn't watching where he's going and runs into the back of my legs where he falls over.

"Geez, lady, that wasn't very nice," Marcus scolds me.

"I didn't do it on purpose. I just now remembered something though." I'm not sure why they still insist on calling me lady. Rabbits are the oddest creatures. But I suspect mine are extra bizarre.

"What did you remember?" Marshall asks. "Did you remember we need more parsley?"

I sigh so loudly a couple walking by stares at me. "Are you ever not thinking about food?" I ask in exasperation, which really causes the couple to stare at me. I just smile, nod my head, and wait for them to move on before addressing the rabbits again.

"I don't suppose the three of you know if Neil Doyle is here today?"

The rabbits then consult with Stumpy while I wait. It's a wonder we don't get thrown out of more places. "Stumpy says he's the guy who's standing by the water fountain, looking at his phone. The one wearing the apron."

"Nice work Stumpy!" I tell him.

"Does that mean we get more treats?" Marcus asks.

I groan. "Just follow me. And don't go anywhere else. We're going home right after this."

Our little caravan approaches Neil at the fountain while getting more odd looks. The locals are used to seeing us around town, but I'm sure we are quite the sight to the tourists.

"Hi, excuse me, Neil?" I ask gently.

Neil looks up from his phone. "Good evening. Is there something I can help you with?"

"Oh, no, I'm not a guest of the hotel or anything. I was just wondering, were you working here last night?"

"Yes, I was."

"Would you be able to tell me which tables you waited on?"

He looks confused at first. "Oh, did you leave something behind? People do that all the time. We have a lost and found box at the front desk."

It didn't even occur to me I should have thought of a good excuse before I questioned him. "Yes, I left, my, um, shoes here."

"Your shoes?"

Drat! That sounded really dumb.

"Yes, and I was sitting near Morley Haynes' table. Was that in your section, by any chance?"

He looks like he smelled something bad. He's clearly not a fan either and I don't blame him after what Shauna told me. "No, I was assigned to that section, but switched with another server. I didn't see any shoes left behind, but like I said, check with the lost and found because they could be there. I have to get to work now, sorry," he mumbles as he hurries away from us.

I watch him walk across the atrium and toward the kitchen for a while before telling the boys it's time to go home.

"Were you questioning him about last night because you're trying to find out who killed Mr. Haynes?" Marcus asks.

"How did you know?"

"Oh, people are talking. It's all over town, you know," Marshall explains.

"I don't doubt that."

"Do you want us to let you know if we hear anything especially juicy?" Marcus asks.

"Yes, please, that would help a lot."

"We'll get extra treats for that, right?"

"Let's just go home."

By the time the four of us get home, I'm so tired it's all I can do to get the boys fed and dinner warmed up in the microwave for me. What a long and trying day. I don't even know if Chloe is still in jail or if she could get out on bail. And then I have all the other people I talked to or heard about today still swirling around in my head.

Right before bed, I scribble down some notes about the case. It's a good thing Drew isn't here. I'd be in trouble for sure. I wish he'd have been a little more forthcoming when I saw him earlier. I know he isn't supposed to talk to us about his cases, but he usually at least gives me a few hints.

Tomorrow I need to see Ethan Davis. Although considering Morley fired him right before he died, I don't know how to track him down. Hopefully, Miranda and Damien will have some ideas. Even though chasing down leads makes Damien nervous, we can usually talk him into helping us.

And then I remember I never started on Damien's letter of recommendation because I was so busy trying to solve a crime. Which I'm not supposed to be doing in the first place. And I don't think we told Drew about their foster parent application, either. I'm the worst friend ever.

Chapter 9

Morning comes too early again. I tossed and turned all night with strange dreams about cupcakes and corpses. I wake up feeling guilty that I didn't write the letter of recommendation for Damien and Tom to become foster parents. What a lousy way to start the day.

I help the boys into the Prius and drive to the cafe all bleary-eyed and grumbly. Damien is already there with the coffee made. "I figured you would need this," he tells me, handing me a steaming cup of joe the moment I walk in the door.

"Bless you, my child," I tell him, grasping the warm mug in my hands, which already makes me feel a bit better. "I feel horrible. I didn't write your letter of recommendation yesterday."

"That's okay. I assume you'll do it today, right?"

"Absolutely, 100%, I will do it today and deliver it. I swear," I hold my hand up like I'm swearing an oath to my dear friend. In a way, I guess I am.

"I should apologize too," Damien starts.

"For what?"

"For giving you such a hard time yesterday about looking into Morley Haynes' murder. You were right when you said I didn't discourage you when you were trying to exonerate my cousin last summer, and now you're just trying to help your friend. I just genuinely worry about you. Next to Tom and Bubbles, you and Miranda are my best friends, and I don't know what I'd do if something happened to you. You've been held at gunpoint twice, and then the last killer threatened to hex you. What you're doing isn't exactly risk free."

"I'm genuinely glad I rank as high as your dog," I respond, laughing.

"You know that's a big deal," Damien laughs along with me.

"I'm not trying to be some kind of private investigator or a cop or anything. It's just that when my friends are accused of a crime, and I feel like I can do something about it, I think I should. And obviously, when I was wrongly accused of murder, I had to step up and protect myself and this cafe."

"I get that. I swear I do," Damien says, putting his hands up in surrender. "Please, just promise me you'll be safe and not put yourself in dangerous situations, okay? At least not until you finish my letter of recommendation, anyway."

"Ha ha, and you're a comedian."

When we hear a knock on the front door, we both turn our heads to look at the old Felix the Cat clock that's hung on the wall since I was a kid. It's 6:30, which means it's Gladys, and she must be chomping at the bit out there.

"It's 6:30!" I exclaim.

"Go! Go! Open the door!" Damiens shouts. "Hurry before she kicks it in!"

Before I can even get out of the kitchen, I concentrate on the lock using my powers to unlock it, so Gladys doesn't need to stand outside in the snow, burrito-less for even one second longer. That makes two days in a row. We're going to hear about it now.

"Sakes alive!" she exclaims as she rushes into the cafe, scraping her boots on the thick doormat and shaking the snow from her coat. "It's cold out there! I was worried you'd found another body or something and weren't opening today. Where would I get my breakfast burrito if that happened?"

Good old Gladys, I don't know what we'd do without her.

"Here you go, Gladys, just for you, one vegan breakfast burrito and a cup of coffee," Damien says as he bursts through the kitchen door out of breath from rushing so fast.

Gladys removes her oversized puffy coat and hat and hangs them on the coat rack. "Did you know Chloe was released on bail last night?" she asks, taking her customary seat in front of the window lest she miss something exciting happening outside.

"I had no idea! I'm glad for that, at least."

"Detective Bailey didn't tell you?"

"No, he stopped by briefly yesterday after Chloe was arrested, but wouldn't tell us anything new. Unfortunately, he just lectured me about keeping out of it."

"I'm sure he's busy with the case," Gladys reassures me.

When Drew is working on a big case, he's laser-focused. I swear, sometimes I even have to remind him to eat.

Once Aranya arrives for her shift, I retire to my office to work on Damien and Tom's recommendation letter. It's an enjoyable break from worrying about what will happen to Chloe if they don't find the real killer.

And even though it looks like whoever really killed Morley did it because they had a personal beef with him, what if that isn't the case?

What if a killer is running free in Crested Peaks, and anyone could be next?

Even one of us? I shiver at the thought and get goosebumps on my arms. Once I finish the letter, I print it out and put it in an envelope for safekeeping. I'll drop it off in person this afternoon, just to be sure.

"It's done!" I proclaim, waving the envelope in the air.

"Thanks, boss!" Damien says. "I can't believe this is actually happening! We could have a kid in our home by Thanksgiving." At that, he turns pale. "We could have a kid in our home by Thanksgiving! We're not ready! I have to baby proof the house! Oh man, what were we thinking?" Damien buries his face in his hands.

I grasp his shoulders. "We will help you! Right, Aranya?"

"Of course!"

"And Miranda too, obviously."

"Okay, you're right," he sighs. "I just have to stay calm. Everything will be fine."

"I'm guessing this is the easy part," I assure him. "The hard part will be when she gets chickenpox, or falls down and skins her knee, or wrecks her bike and needs stitches—"

"—what?" Damien shouts. "Those kinds of things don't actually happen, do they? I'll completely freak out if they do."

Oh boy, me and my big mouth. "I'm sure you guys will figure it out as you go along. Why don't you sit down and take a break. Just a few deep breaths, that's it. I'll make you a nice cup of tea," I tell him as I guide him to a chair so he can stop for a moment and calm down. I think he gets nervous when Miranda and I are off on one of our adventures. A kid will send him right over the edge.

"Anybody home?"

"What's Drew doing here?" I ask Damien.

"He's your boyfriend, maybe?" Damien responds.

"I don't mean that. I'm worried he has bad news. I wasn't expecting him."

"Well, go see!" Damien insists, pushing me out the door.

"This is a nice surprise!" I tell him. "At least I hope so..." I trail off.

"I have come to take you to lunch if you're free!"

I turn to Damien and Aranya. "Go! Go!" Aranya urges, making sweeping motions with her hands.

"Okay," I respond, taking off my apron and hanging it from its hook. "Oh! Wait!" I hold up a finger to Drew before I dash into the back and grab the recommendation letter. "I have to drop this off!" I tell him.

"At the post office?" he asks. Obviously confused by the lack of address or stamp on the front.

"It's a surprise, and I'll tell you on the way there," I grin and glance back at Damien, who's grinning back.

"Uh oh, what now?" Drew asks.

"It's not an uh oh, you curmudgeon. It's good news, I swear."

"Okayyyy," he responds, looking extremely skeptical.

"She's serious this time. It's good news," Damien assures him.

"Okay, I believe you, Damien."

Like I've ever misled him about something! Okay, so maybe a few things, but not that many.

"Can we run over to the Health and Human Services department before lunch? It will only take a moment."

Now Drew looks alarmed. "What do you need at DHHS? Tell me what's going on right now. You're worrying me."

"Damien and Tom are applying to become foster parents."

"No way! Are you serious? That's fantastic!"

"I know! He asked me to write a letter of recommendation for them, and that's what I need to drop off now."

"I know the Director over there. CPPD works with them whenever we encounter a child at risk. I'll call her this afternoon and tell her what outstanding parents Tom and Damien will be. Have they told them if they already have someone in mind for them?"

"Yes! It's a three-year-old girl named Poppy and that would be so great of you to talk to them. I know Damien will be thrilled to hear it."

"I'm happy to do it. And I'm so excited for them."

"The little girl's mother died, and they're trying to find a family member, but so far no luck. Sounds like Damien and Tom are willing to adopt her if that becomes an option."

"So it's a celebratory lunch!" Drew declares.

Unfortunately, the DHHS offices are deserted when we arrive. Turns out they're eating lunch at the same time we are. But I put my letter in the middle of the receptionist's desk where she's sure to see it when she gets back. Drew says when he talks to the Director today, he'll make sure she sees it.

We stop at Sam's Sandwich Shop, which is crowded but luckily, we snatch a table just as someone else is leaving. Drew orders the sandwich of the day, a Ricotta, Marmalade, and Salami sandwich which I've never even heard of. It's rosemary focaccia with orange marmalade spread on one side and ricotta on the other, then layered with thin-sliced fennel salami.

I pick the Spinach-Artichoke with Havarti Cheese sandwich. Two slices of thick, multigrain bread, spread with cream cheese and then topped with thinly sliced marinated artichoke hearts, spinach, and dill pickles, finished off with havarti cheese.

Sam's has the best sandwiches in town. We split a basket of their special kettle potato chips that are made fresh every morning while I top it all off with an Isolation Ale, a locally brewed seasonal beer. I'm the boss, so I can have a beer with lunch if I want. Drew can't drink because he's still on duty.

"Is there anything new about Chloe's case that you can tell me?" I plead. "Gladys said she made bail, but I haven't seen her yet."

"You won't like this because I know she's your friend—"

"—and she's innocent!"

Drew sighs. I know he thinks I'm always tilting at windmills with these cases. I understand he looks strictly at the facts and evidence in front of him. Still, I always remember what it was like to be falsely accused of murder. I just know some people who are innocent, no matter what the evidence shows.

"What I'm about to tell you isn't public knowledge. When we searched Chloe's truck, we found an empty syringe. The lab tested it, and it had traces of cyanide in it. The same poison that killed Morley. That, combined with her history with him, was enough to arrest her."

Suddenly my sandwich doesn't taste as good as it did a few seconds ago. "Cyanide?" I whisper as I feel the blood drain from my face. "That's just not possible. I swear to you, there's no way Chloe did it. How would she even have access to something like cyanide?"

Drew tries to take my hand, but I pull it back. Can't he see? I know Chloe, and she would never hurt someone, much less poison them with cyanide in one of her own cupcakes.

"Charlotte, this is the evidence we have in front of us. Of course, we're still investigating because we have to build a solid case, but all signs point to Chloe. There's even some speculation that she used her enhanced decorations on the cupcake, and a special recipe, to hide the poison."

"Enhanced?" I hiss. "You mean because she uses witchcraft to decorate the cupcakes that automatically makes her suspicious."

"I didn't say I was the one pushing that theory. In fact, I've emphasized that her magic has nothing to do with it. If she poisoned him, we need to look strictly at the facts and not speculate on her ability to use witchcraft."

"But why would a murderer poison someone and then leave the evidence behind in their own food truck?" my voice cracks with emotion.

"We've had this discussion before Char, criminals don't always act logically."

"She's not a criminal!" I insist, and now I'm even more upset because people are staring at us.

"She may have kept it intending to destroy it later, and we caught her before she could do it. I don't know. I do know that the syringe was in her cupcake truck and had her fingerprints all over it."

"What about Shauna?" I blurt out. "And all the others?"

"Well, that came out of left field. What do you mean, what about Shauna and all the others?"

"When we talked to her yesterday, she said after she told Morley, at the Halloween Festival, that she wished he was dead, she went back to work. How do we know that's even true?" I know I'm grasping at straws at this point and that I'm about to get in trouble for admitting that I've questioned potential suspects, but I don't care. I'm desperate.

"Shauna told *us*, the proper authorities, the same thing. *And* she turned over her computer logs to the CPPD proving that she was working, as she said she was, at the time of Morley's death."

"Oh," is the only thing I can think of to say.

"Have you questioned others?" he asks.

"No!"

"Are you planning to question others?"

My silence is a dead giveaway.

"How many times do we need to have this discussion, Char? You can't keep doing this."

"I need to know that the CPPD is looking at every possible suspect and not just Chloe. A lot of people hated Morley. Like, really, really, hated the guy. Not just Chloe."

"I promise you I'm doing my job. And we're examining all the evidence we have, so you don't need to worry."

Drew won't like this, but I have to step up my investigation double time. I know Chloe didn't do this, and I don't care what they found in her truck. But if the CPPD likes her for this, then I'll need to talk to the other suspects on my own. My friend's freedom relies on it.

Chapter 10

Once again, I trudge back to Marcall's after lunch, my feet feeling as heavy as the rest of me. I just can't understand how Chloe ended up with a poisonous syringe in her truck. It makes zero sense.

"Uh oh, what happened?" Damiens asks the minute he sees my face. "Did they say something to you at the foster office?"

"What? Oh, no, it's not that at all! In fact, I may have good news about that!"

"Then why so glum?" Aranya asks.

"Drew said they found an empty syringe with traces of cyanide in Chloe's Cupcake truck, and that's the poison that was in the cupcake that killed Morley."

"What?" Damien exclaims. "That's not possible."

"That's exactly what I said. And now I'm worried that with evidence like that, they won't be looking at anyone else."

"That's really rough." Damien shakes his head sorrowfully. "Can I ask, though, what the good news is? Since it's about our foster application, maybe?"

"First, I dropped off the letter. They were all out to lunch as well, but I put it in the middle of the receptionist's desk so she can't miss it. Second, Drew actually knows the director and is going to call her this afternoon and tell her how utterly fabulous you are."

"Oh Charlotte, that's amazing. I can't thank you, or Drew, enough for that. Can you believe it? We may have a little girl very soon."

"I'm sorry for being down about Chloe with all the other hopeful news. It's just so hard to imagine. I need to do something."

"Let's go talk to Ethan," Damien suggests.

"Morley's employee?"

"Yep," he nods his head.

"You're seriously suggesting that we investigate this?"

"I feel like I owe you, so yes, let's go. However, I see even a hint of a gun, and I'm tearing out of there so fast you'll forget I ever mentioned it."

I giggle. "Okay, I'm good with that. And for the record, it's usually just the bad guy who pulls a gun on me. Not everybody I talk to threatens to kill me."

"What if Ethan turns out to be the killer, though?"

"Seriously, what are the odds that someone will hold me hostage at gunpoint for a *third* time?"

"You just had to say that, didn't you?" Damien says in disbelief.

"Aranya, are you okay by yourself for a while? It should be pretty quiet now until we close."

Aranya waves her hand at us. "I'm good! You guys go do what you have to."

Damien and I grab our coats and head out into the cold afternoon. It's starting to snow again, but it's still just a light dusting of snowflakes. The Halloween themed lights shine out underneath the snow, making the whole area glow.

After several steps, I laugh out loud.

"What's so funny?" Damien asks.

"Do we even know where we're going? I was so caught up in the moment I forgot to ask!"

Damien looks at me like I'm losing it. "We're going to the mortuary. Where else would we go to talk to Morley's assistant?"

"But Morley fired him last night," I point out.

Now, Damien is the one laughing. "Morley fires him all the time. I guarantee, especially now that Morley is dead, Ethan is there working today."

"Okay, I hope you're right about this. Otherwise, we walked all this way in the snow for nothing." I'm still not convinced that someone who got fired would just turn up again at work the next day like nothing had happened.

I breathe a sigh of relief when we walk into the mortuary and a blast of warm air hits us. "Here comes Ethan," Damien whispers. "Also, I told you so."

"Good afternoon, is there something I can help you folks with? Are you looking to pre-purchase burial plots? A lot of couples are doing it. It's one less burden for your children after you pass."

I look down at Damien and try not to guffaw. What a funny-looking couple we'd make.

"As a matter of fact, that's exactly why we're here!" Damien says.

"It is?"

"Oh, honey, there's no need to be nervous. Remember, it's for the kids," he coos as he reaches up to take my hand. Oh dear, I'm not sure where he's going with this, but I guess I'll have to play along.

Ethan leads us to a small table where we sit side by side. "You folks make yourselves comfortable while I gather the literature. My name is Ethan Davis, and I'll be assisting you. Can I get you something to drink?"

"I'd love a cup of coffee if you don't mind," Damien tells him.

"Coming right up, sir!"

After he rushes off to get Damien some coffee, I whisper, "I assume you have a plan here?"

He pats my hand. "Of course I do. Just play along."

He returns in a matter of seconds with an entire serving tray complete with delicately patterned teacups, sugar, and cream, along with a small pot of coffee. He sets it down in front of us and then rushes off again. I assume this time to get the paperwork.

Damien picks up the small pot, examining it carefully. "Do you suppose this is any good?" he asks. He's a total coffee snob. If it just happens to be coffee that came from a machine and a small plastic cup, I'm going to have fun watching him try to drink it.

Ethan returns with a stack of notebooks and brochures in his hands, settling down in a chair across from us. "Okay, folks, here are some brochures for you to take home and look over, but I also have our plans laid out in detail just in case you're looking to purchase today." He stacks several three-ring binders in front of us. Each with laminated pages showing different caskets, urns, and headstones.

"Have you folks thought about what might be best for you? Some customers come in here with very set ideas in mind, while others are open to anything. We're fine with whatever makes you the happiest."

Damien leans forward to address Ethan, his hand on one knee, an elbow on the other. Very convincing if you ask me. "Let me be honest with you, Ethan." I choke on my coffee a little at this point. "We were at the Halloween Festival when your boss died right in front of us."

Ethan pales slightly. "Oh, I'm so sorry to hear about that. I'm sorry you had to see it."

"Actually, I think it was a good thing." Damien points his finger at Ethan. He's really getting into this. "It opened our eyes to the fact that you never know when it's your time. And we want to make arrangements in advance so our family doesn't have to deal with it, should we pass unexpectedly like Mr. Haynes."

"That's why our customers love our pre-paid plans," he says, nodding his head. "Assuming you've lived a long and happy life, once you pass, your children won't be burdened with the costs of a funeral or even a burial plot."

"Forgive me," I tell him as soon as I realize where we're going with this, "we haven't even offered our condolences for *your* loss."

"Oh. Well, here's the thing. Can you keep a secret?"

"Definitely!" Damien and I say simultaneously.

Ethan smiles. "You make such a cute couple." At this, I roll my eyes so hard I think I pulled something. "Mr. Haynes was not the - how should I say this - nicest man in the world."

I nod my head vigorously. "I've heard that. In fact, we even heard Mr. Haynes fired you on Halloween, so we're a little surprised to see you here now."

Ethan looks like he's caught off guard for just a moment and I'm waiting for him to ask who could have told us, while I franticly try to decide which name I could throw out that would sound credible. "He actually fired me all the time."

"No way!" Damien responds.

"Like I said, he wasn't a very nice man, and that's putting it mildly." He chuckles, "Okay, I admit it, I couldn't stand the guy."

Damien and I stare at him without responding. Drew told me that was a police technique, although if he realized I'd use it for actual, uh, unauthorized police work, I'm sure he wouldn't have shared that tidbit. People like to talk about themselves, and silence often makes others uncomfortable. So they fill it with details and stories. Ethan seems like the perfect experiment for this.

As I predicted, he interprets our silence as a reason to continue. First, he looks around to make sure no one else is listening. "I know it's rude to speak ill of the dead, but I for one am glad he's gone. I would even bet that a lot of people are." He puts his finger against his lips. "Don't tell anybody I said that, okay? Kudos to that cupcake chick for finally doing what the rest of us had only dreamed of." Then he giggles. "Oops, did I just say that out loud?" He leans in closer, "By the way does anybody know how she did it? I'm dying to know."

Damien opens his mouth to answer, but when I put my hand over his, he stops. When I talked to Drew, he said the cause of death wasn't public knowledge. And while I may be willing to interview suspects, even though I'm not supposed to, I feel like betraying his confidence would be stepping way over the line.

"I heard he once lost a body in Cripple Creek because he stopped to gamble, and someone stole the hearse." I bring up, hoping to distract him.

"That was the saddest thing ever. That poor old man. Actually, if anyone was going to kill Haynes, I figured it would be Owen Munoz. Morley even had to get a restraining order against him, it got so bad. Even if he didn't kill him, I'm sure he's celebrating these days. We'll probably see him spit on his grave or something, he hated him so much. Although I don't blame him." Ethan shudders, and I almost expect to see him throw salt over his shoulder.

"I daresay he's the most unlikeable man in Crested Peaks. Or he was anyway." He laughs at his own joke. Damien and I laugh along with him, of course, because we want him to keep talking. Actually, if he'd just admit he killed his boss right here and now, we could be done with all of this, but I've learned that unfortunately, it's never that easy.

He leans in even closer. "Can I tell you folks another little secret?"

"Yes!" we reply again in unison. I glare at Damien. We have to stop doing that.

Ethan smiles. "Morley was grooming me to take over the business so he could retire."

"Really?" I ask. This time, fortunately, without Damien's help.

He nods his head vigorously. "He considered me a manager in training," he boasts, making air quotes. "As soon as he felt I was properly trained, he was retiring and leaving the entire business to me!" He exclaims, poking himself in the chest in case we didn't realize exactly who he was talking about.

"How long have you been in training?" I ask. I didn't know Morley, obviously, but it seems odd that someone would repeatedly fire a person they intended to take over the business.

"Four years!" he says proudly.

"Oh! Does it take that long to learn to run a mortuary?"

His face falters. "Well, no, not really. I already have a degree in Business Management and a Funeral Director's license, but he wanted to make sure I was especially well trained before he stepped back."

"So now that Morley is dead, does that mean you automatically become the General Manager? Since you were already training for that?" Damien asks.

He looks around again to triple check no one is listening in. "I'm assuming that's what will happen. Everyone knew I was being trained to take over, and I'm sure that Morley had that covered in his will. It's just a matter of time before the lawyer locates that and makes me General Manager."

"Well, congratulations then!" Damien tells him. "I mean, under the circumstances."

Ethan assumes the appropriate serious facial expression. "Yes, yes, of course. A tragedy in some respects, but perhaps better for all involved in the long run. And gosh, I feel bad now. I'm supposed to go over all these materials with you folks, but I ended up talking all about me!"

Damien pats him on the hand. "You know, that's fine, given that we only recently decided to do this. Why don't we take home some of your literature home, talk it over, and then we'll get back to you after we've made a decision."

"Marvelous!" Ethan claps his hand together. "Let me just give you these, and please don't hesitate to call us with any questions." He walks us to the front door, where we can see it's snowing harder now. "Bundle up, you guys. It's cold out there! We'll be in touch!"

"By the way," I stop right before opening the door. "Were you at the hotel that night for the party? That would have been hard for you to see, I imagine. Morley dying, I mean."

"Nah, I left after we argued, and he fired me. I picked up some takeout for dinner, then went home and passed out candy to the kids who were trick or treating."

"Thanks for your help, we'll be in touch," Damien tells him as we head out into the bitterly cold mountain air. I pull my heavy hood up over my head while sliding thick mittens over my hands. It's windier, and the snow is coming down heavier than when we first walked into the mortuary. It's uncomfortable to walk in, but the more it snows, the better it is for skiing, and the runoff in the spring will mean more water for the area.

"When did you come up with that whole scenario? Have you been plotting that this entire time?"

Damien does this weird skipping thing while smacking me on the arm. He's so proud of himself. "Ha! I thought of that as we were walking in! Was that awesome or what?" he says, laughing at himself. "And you did a good job playing along!"

"So, what did you think of his story?" I ask while watching Damien bob and weave around the sidewalk like he's some kind of prizefighter. For a guy who typically tries to talk us out of these kinds of things, he's having a good time now.

"I think he could have killed Haynes. Considering he had every reason to hate the guy, and it didn't seem like Morley was letting him become General Manager anytime soon, he had a great excuse for getting him out of the way, right? Hey, have you had any of those psychic thingamajiggies like you had when Darla was murdered?"

Last summer when Darla, who was Damien's cousin's girlfriend, was murdered, I experienced several instances where I knew that one of the suspects was lying about something. It wasn't a gut feeling; it was way more powerful than that. Turns out the suspect was secretly Darla's father, but not the murderer.

Miranda thinks I may have some limited psychic abilities that I could have inherited from my grandma or even my parents. Unfortunately, it's too late now to know for sure.

"Miranda asked me the same thing after we talked to Shauna. My answer is still no, I haven't experienced any psychic thingamajiggies, as you say, since last summer and all the drama with Cody.

"I wish I could get some kind of reading though. It would make this all go a lot faster. But I agree, Morley seems like the type of guy who claims he was going to hand over the reigns to his eager assistant, while leaving him overworked and underpaid with no intention of ever making him manager." I surmise.

"And with Morley dead," Damien adds, "that paves the way for Ethan to take over."

"Except he said he left the party and went home."

"That's a pretty weak alibi," Damien points out.

"Would he have access to cyanide is another question we need answered," I remind him.

"We can't forget Owen Munoz," Damien points out. "The only thing we know so far is why he hated Morley, but we didn't actually talk to him specifically about the night Morley was killed."

I stop in the middle of the sidewalk in shock. "Damien Torres, are you offering to question yet another suspect with me?"

He shakes his head. "It's getting a little late, and Tom is expecting me. We're working on getting the house kid proofed tonight. If they approve our written application, then they'll do a home visit, so we have to be ready for that."

"I wonder if Drew talked to the director yet?" I ask.

"I've been thinking about it all afternoon!"

"C'mon, let's go back to the cafe and call him. It's too cold to keep standing around out here."

Chapter 11

We hurry back into the cafe, relieved to feel the warm air on our faces again.

"Hey, guys!" Aranya greets us. "I wasn't sure you'd make it back before we closed."

"Damien here was busy picking out burial plots for us."

"Er, what?"

Damien laughs. "Our boss is referring to my brilliant acting abilities and plan to get information out of Ethan Davis without making him suspicious."

"I admit, it was a pretty good plan."

"By the way, Miranda stopp-"

Miranda bursts through the door as usual before Aranya can finish her sentence. "Hey you two! Aranya said you went to the mortuary. Did you get anything good? She also said the police found a syringe with cyanide in it in Chloe's truck. I don't believe it for a second. No way, no how."

"How much coffee have you had today?" I ask.

"A lot! Why?" Miranda hovers in the doorway, stomping her feet and rubbing her hands together for warmth.

"Come inside, so we don't all freeze to death, and we'll tell you what happened. How many hot chocolates should I make?" Aranya giggles when everyone throws their hand in the air. "Okay, four."

"Do you need help, boss?" she asks. Damien likes to call me boss, which was kind of weird at first, but then I decided it was mostly endearing. But now he has Aranya calling me boss as well. Whatever happened to just Charlotte? I'm afraid to say anything because I don't want them to think I'm mad. Things I never realized I'd have to deal with before I inherited my Gran's cafe. That and all the dead bodies.

"Nope! I'm good." I duck into the kitchen to prepare the hot chocolate for my friends. Miranda has been helping me with potion work lately. It's actually a difficult skill to master, and I much prefer practical skills like making objects move, but I can see where it would come in handy sometimes. And if it helps me make delicious hot chocolate, then even better.

Damien always lectures me on the importance of mise en place - getting all the ingredients out and ready before I cook - which I admit is often difficult for me to remember. I much prefer the 'get one thing out at a time, only to discover I'm completely out of the last ingredient, and have to go to the store to get it' method. And yes, I admit it, Damien's way creates much less stress in my life, but it also requires discipline I don't always have.

I work on levitating several ingredients to the work table all at once, which requires a great deal of concentration. It really bugs me when I mess up and drop something. Thankfully, I move everything to the worktable without breaking anything this time. I've got everything I need: almond milk, cocoa powder, sugar, dark chocolate chips, vanilla

— rats — I don't have any vanilla extract. Okay, almond extract will add something different here.

But when I begin to pour in a teaspoon of almond extract, I'm hit with a powerful, all-knowing wave of energy and I realize without a doubt that the secret ingredient in Chloe's red velvet cupcakes is almond extract. That may also be why the real killer used it, because the cyanide would smell like almonds and mask any potential suspicion. I really wish I could control these kinds of revelations, because that would be far more useful than having them just pop up now and again.

I put the milk, cocoa powder, and sugar in a saucepan. Oops spilled a little milk. Okay, breathe and concentrate, you got this. Strange as it may seem, I find that using magic to hurl objects at a bad guy, is easier than using that same magic to add ingredients to a small pan in such a precise manner. Once everything is combined, I add the chocolate chips.

"Everything all right in there?" Miranda calls out.

"It's all good!" I yell back. "Just trying to do it all with magic and trying not to spill anything!"

"Good girl!" she says.

When everything is melted and heated properly, I add in just a bit of potion that I created recently that's supposed to bring some good cheer to those who drink it. I figure we can all use that right now.

Then I really get wild and levitate all four drinks on a tray out the door.

"Wow!" Damien whistles. "Well done!"

I breathe a sigh of relief and take a little bow. My friends are all well aware of my background. For most of my life, I denied my magic heritage. I was convinced that was the best way to ensure I didn't turn out like my parents. Crooks. Once I got back to Crested Peaks though and met so many wonderful people, I realized witchcraft had nothing to do with my parents being horrible people.

But I'm also finding I have a lot of work to catch up on. Thankfully, Miranda has been a huge help in this area and gets after me to practice my new skills regularly. Sometimes I forget I can use them for more than just fending off gun-wielding maniacs.

"What do we have so far?" Miranda asks when I finally take a seat with the rest of them.

I start. "Unfortunately, the worst news is that police found a syringe with traces of cyanide in Chloe's cupcake truck."

"There's no way!" Miranda responds in anger.

I put my hands up. "That's what Drew said."

"I don't care what they found. There's no way Chloe killed Morley. Sure, I bet there were times when she wanted to punch him right in the face, but she'd never kill someone."

"I agree, and that's why we're investigating this, because I don't think the police are doing very much to look beyond Chloe. And now I have something else to tell you." They all stop mid-sip expecting some huge revelation. "The secret ingredient in Chloe's red velvet cupcakes is almond extract."

"Cyanide can smell like almonds," Aranya points out.

"Exactly," I nod my head.

Miranda gasps. "You had a reading."

"I did."

"And?" Damien prompts.

"And what? That was it."

"That doesn't seem very helpful," he tells me.

"It may be later on, you know!" I retort.

"So we have Shauna shouting at Morley that she wished he were dead, right before he actually dies, and who then tells us very plainly that she's glad he died." Aranya reminds us.

"And then I ran into Neil last night when I had to pick up Marshall, Marcus, and Stumpy from the Hotel Glacier," I tell them.

"You did?" Miranda asks.

"I swear I was there solely to track down my wayward critters, and there he was, right in front of me."

"What did he say?" Aranya asks. "Was it similar to what Shauna said?"

"Uh, well, I didn't exactly admit who I was, or that I had just talked to Shauna that day."

"I'm shocked," Damien retorts.

"Hey!" I say, pointing at him. "I'm not the one who made up a whole story about us needing couple's burial plots!"

"What?" Miranda laughs.

"You won't believe what he told Ethan," I explain. "But first, I told Neil I lost my shoes-"

"-your shoes?" Damien asks.

"Will you let me finish? It was all I could come up with on the spur of the moment. I told him I was sitting near Morley's table and must have left my shoes behind. I also asked him if he waited on Morley's table that night, but he said no and that he switched with another server."

"And now we get to my part," Damien says. "I suggested that we pay a visit to Ethan Davis at the mortuary."

"It was your idea?" Miranda asks in shock. "You hate that we do this."

"I know, but I felt like I owed Charlotte one, so I suggested we go over there and talk to him."

"I thought Morley fired him, though. Why was he at the mortu-ary?"

"Oh, just wait," I tell her.

Then Damien proceeds to fill the other two in on that afternoon's escapade at the mortuary. I think Miranda and Aranya were a mixture of horrified and amused that he would make up such a wild story and then play it off so well.

Miranda ticks the suspects off on her fingers. "So far, all have will-ingly and loudly admitted to being treated like crap by Morley."

"Right," I respond.

"I still don't think we should overlook Owen Munoz either, though," Damien points out.

"Does anyone know where to find him?" I ask. I'm dumbfounded when none of them know. "Seriously? Every single time I've wanted to talk to a suspect, one of you has always known when and where they are!"

"I'm at a loss this time," Miranda says with a shrug.

"Me too boss," Damien adds.

I glance at Aranya. "Don't look at me. I'm new to this crazy game, remember?"

"Okay, so I guess the next task on our list is to figure out how to find Owen."

Damien glances down at his phone when it rings and immediately starts to sweat. "Oh no, it's DHHS!"

"Well, answer it!" I tell him.

"What do I say? What if they're calling to say they're rejecting our application?"

"You don't know until you answer it!" I snap.

"Okay, okay," he takes a deep breath, "hello, this is Damien Torres. Uh huh, uh huh, okay, sure, no problem, thank you."

When he hangs up for one awful second, I'm convinced it was bad news. He looks kind of pale and like he's about to throw up.

"The director said after the glowing recommendation from Detective Bailey, they're fast-tracking our application and want to do the home visit tomorrow."

Damien may have been so nervous he might throw up, but the rest of us explode in celebration.

He claps his hands against his face. "Do you realize how much we have to do before tomorrow?" he moans.

"You better go home and get started then," I insist.

"And I'll cover for you tomorrow! What time are they coming?" Aranya asks.

"11:30," he squeaks.

"Plenty of time to get everything ready if you leave now," I urge him. "Go! Get out of here and don't come back until you've been approved!"

"Okay, yeah, thanks!" Damien mumbles as he grabs his coat and things and races for the door. Just as he opens the door, he pauses. "I don't know how I'll ever be able to thank you enough, every one of you."

"Thank us by leaving!" Miranda shouts.

And with that, he's out the door, racing past the window on his way to the parking lot.

"Ten bucks says he barfs on the social worker's shoes tomorrow," Miranda says.

"Oh, I think that's a given," I respond.

Chapter 12

After that, there isn't much to add, so I levitate our dirty cups back to the kitchen area while Miranda and Aranya head out into the cold snowstorm. I gather the three boys who are thankfully sound asleep in my office and not out in the snow looking for treats.

The roads are slippery enough that I drive home extra cautiously as I continue to ponder a way to find Mr. Munoz. Just as I'm pulling into my driveway, my phone rings. It's Chloe!

"Hey, Chloe!" I answer. "Where are you? Are you okay?"

"I'm at home. I was released on bail, as I'm sure you've already heard through the Crested Peaks gossip hotline," she sighs. She sounds tired. I know what it's like to have a cloud of suspicion hanging over your head. When my former landlord was murdered behind my cafe, the police found the weapon in the park up the street. Unfortunately, it came from my cafe, and had my fingerprints all over it.

"Is there anything I can do for you?" I ask.

"I kind of feel like getting out of the house. Are you doing anything tonight? You want to go out to dinner or something?"

"Here's an idea. Why don't you come over to my place and I'll cook dinner for you. I'll make a fire, we can just hang out, drink some wine, and watch a movie if you want."

"That actually sounds really good," she responds with a sigh of relief.

"Okay, give me an hour to feed the boys their dinner, and then get everything else ready."

"That sounds great. I'll see you in a bit."

I touch the phone screen to hang up. I just hope I can help her because so far, it's looking really bad for her.

Precisely an hour later, the doorbell rings. "Chloe's here!" the rabbits shout.

"Let her in!" I call back laughing. The confused looks on their faces when I say that never gets old for me.

I open the door and realize it's snowing even harder now. "It's really starting to come down out there!" she exclaims as she bustles into the house.

"I'm so sorry, Chloe." I give her a big hug before she can even get her coat off.

"Thank you," she whispers. "I appreciate all your support."

"I guess I should let you come in now," I say, finally letting her go. "Take off your coat and go warm up in front of the fireplace while I pour some wine."

"What did you bring us?" Marcus asks, standing at her feet, blocking her way.

"She didn't bring you anything. She has far more important things to worry about than your treats. Now step aside so she can come in."

"Actually," she says, "I brought them some of these." When she reaches into her pocket and pulls out a couple of blueberries, their eyes nearly bug out of their heads. They love blueberries. She holds them out in the palm of her hand as they each grab one and race off, flopping down in front of their fireplace to enjoy their newfound treasures.

"And I didn't forget you, Stumpy," she tells him as he eagerly awaits at her feet now that he realizes they're getting presents. "It's a cookie from the Five Dachshund Bakery."

"Oh, he loves those!" I tell her.

Stumpy snatches his treat from her hand as well and settles himself down on the couch to gnaw on it. Nothing like cat treat crumbs all over the sofa.

As I hang up Chloe's coat, I tell her to make herself at home while I pour us each a large glass of white wine. "I have tomato soup and grilled cheese panini if that sounds good to you," I tell her. "Whenever you're ready to eat."

"This is all fabulous. Thank you so much. You shouldn't have gone to all this trouble. I could have just brought takeout over."

"It's really no big deal, just soup and sandwiches." Then I jump right in. "So, what's the deal with the syringe in your cupcake truck? I don't understand that."

Chloe takes a deep and jagged breath, and for a moment, I'm sure she's going to cry. I know I'm just throwing this at her with no small talk. Still, it seems weird to waste time chatting about the upcoming ski season when she's accused of murdering her former boss.

"You know how much I hated that guy Charlotte."

"I do."

"He's the reason I started the cupcake business to begin with! I loved cosmetology, and I felt like I was providing a valuable service to people. I know it must sound weird, but for some people, I brought them a little peace. Like the family of the young man who was in a horrible car accident. I could put him back together enough to have an open casket funeral and make him look natural. It meant a lot to his family to see him like that. I can't bring their loved one back, but I can at least do *something* for them."

I nod my head at her, unable to really add anything to the conversation at this point. I saw many crappy things in my life thanks to my unsavory parents, but I can't imagine what some people go through when a loved one dies too young.

"I hated that Morley was such a horrible person and made working for him a living hell. And yes, I could have moved somewhere and taken a job at another mortuary, but I didn't want to leave Crested Peaks just because of him."

"So, you started your own business."

"I took my love for baking and serving others, and I started a business, yes," she smiles.

"Now *that* I understand. And in case you were wondering, I have yet to come across a single person who has the slightest good thing to say about him."

"I don't doubt that," she shakes her head sadly. "But I swear to you Charlotte, I never would have killed him."

"I know you wouldn't."

"And I have no idea how that syringe got into my truck."

"This may sound obvious, but you lock the door, right?"

"I always lock the door, but..." she trails off.

Uh oh. "But what?"

"When I got to the truck, the morning after Morley died, I noticed the door was unlocked, when I knew for a fact I had locked it when I left the night before."

"Oh no, did you call the police?"

From the look on her face, she clearly didn't. "My first thought was the condition of my truck inside. I worried someone broke in and vandalized it overnight or stole something. Some of that equipment is incredibly expensive, you know..."

I'm nauseous because I can just picture where this is going.

"I went into the truck terrified of what I might see, but when it looked like nothing had been touched, I was so relieved. I assumed that whoever picked the lock had changed their minds, or when they realized there wasn't any money in the truck, they left." She throws her hands up in defeat and looks so heartbroken I want to cry.

"And then you just went on about your business," I add, almost in a whisper.

"Right, I had cupcakes to make and customers to serve. I planned to let the police know later, but then next thing I know, they're knocking on my door and arresting me."

I take an extra big gulp of wine. "And when you tried to tell them about the lock being picked—"

"—it was too late. They didn't believe me. I just don't know what to do. I have a lawyer, but it all seems so hopeless. I'm going to lose the food truck and go to jail, all because of that monster Morley. I should have just moved away." Chloe then drops her head into her hands and sobs.

I gently rub her back and just let her have a good cry. She's obviously been holding back, and I think it's good for her to let it all out. When she finally stops, I take her hand. "You have to know that you have a lot of friends here in Crested Peaks, and not a single one of us thinks you could have done this. And I promise you, I'm doing everything I can to help clear your name."

"Really?" she sniffles. "Are you even supposed to be helping with this? As much as I appreciate the help, I don't want you to get in trouble with the CPPD or anything."

"Don't worry about a thing," I wave my hand in dismissal. "So far I've talked to Shauna, and her boyfriend Neil, and Ethan at the mortuary, about their relationship with Morley and where they were that night."

"Seriously? You think one of them could have killed him?"

"Given the lengthy list of people who hated him, it seems like just about anyone in this town could have. But I'm trying to narrow down the list to people who had the most reason to hate him and who also had access to him that night. And then there's the pesky detail of who could have had access to the cyanide. But one step at a time."

"Is there any way I can help? I can't believe you're doing this for me, Charlotte. I'm so grateful."

"I know better than anybody what it's like to be falsely accused of committing a crime, so I'm happy to help in any way that I can. Besides, your cupcakes are delicious, and we can't afford to lose them."

"They are rather delicious, aren't they?" she laughs. "What did Shauna say when you talked to her? Haynes was downright emotionally abusive to her mother, and Shauna hates him."

"Yes, she made that perfectly clear. She mentioned that she heard they arrested you and that she was glad you killed him. She also wished she had thought to do that herself a long time ago."

"She actually said that to you?" Chloe responds in shock.

"She actually did."

"Wow. Did you know that the trust her mom set up for her is worth a ton of money?"

"Define ton."

"I'm not sure exactly, but I've heard rumors that it could be as high as $200,000."

"That's a lot of money."

"But here's the real kicker. The original trust was established, so Shauna automatically got the money when she turned 28. But rumor also has it that Morley got some shady lawyer to rewrite the terms, making him the manager of the trust."

My mouth drops open. "Morley took her money?"

"Not exactly, although I'm sure he tried. I think the best he could do was set it up so he had control of her mom's money."

"Now that Morley's dead, does Shauna finally get the money? Or does she still have to wait until she's 28? $200,000 is a lot of money, but is it worth killing over? Especially if you assume she would get the money eventually no matter what."

Chloe shrugs. "That part I don't know for sure."

"How do you know all this?"

"I worked for the mortuary, remember? We know all sorts of people's secrets. Families get very emotional and tell stories while they're with us. I never actually repeated any of those secrets until now though, just so you know."

"Which leads me to the next person I talked to, Ethan Davis."

At this, Chloe laughs.

"What, what's so funny?"

"I know it really isn't funny, but that poor guy, I don't know what his deal is. Morley was horrible to him, too. Fired him all the time, but then Ethan would sweet talk him and beg him to let him come back and Morley would relent. I swear he did it just for fun. He loved to lord his power over Ethan."

"Morley fired him at the Halloween Festival. They had a big fight about it in front of everyone, from what I hear. But he was back at work today."

"That's Ethan. Just keep showing up to work no matter what."

"He said Morley was training him to become the General Manager at the mortuary when he retired."

This time Chloe snorts. "Morley was never retiring, and he was never making Ethan a manager. Yet another one of his sick games. Man, that guy was messed up."

"You're sure of that? Because Ethan is convinced that he really was becoming the manager. And now that Morley is dead, he's extra convinced of it."

"I swear to you, Charlotte, there is no way Ethan was ever taking over that mortuary. I don't care what Morley told him. He'd have to pry that mortuary out of Morley Haynes cold dead hands."

"So Morley's poisoning could be his best chance?" I ask.

"It would have to be."

"And there's another person I think we should talk to, Owen Munoz."

"Oh yeah, that poor guy. You weren't here when that happened, were you?"

"I wasn't, but he showed up at Marcall's the day after Morley died, and when he saw the story in the newspaper, he practically danced a jig. And made no effort to hide it."

"Did he tell you he sued Morley?"

"No, he didn't mention that. What happened? Did he win?"

"The jury found Morley guilty of negligence but only awarded Mr. Munoz the cost of the funeral."

"All he got was a free funeral out of it?"

"Yeah, they said that Morley was at fault for leaving the hearse unattended, but the teens were responsible for the actual damage to his wife's body. Morley considered it a win for himself and threw it in Mr. Munoz face every chance he got."

"That guy was really a piece of work, wasn't he?"

"Imagine working for him all those years!"

"Owen was so distraught he showed up at the mortuary one day, jumped Morley in the parking lot, and tried to beat him up."

"What?" I shriek.

"It took several employees to pull him off Morley. And then at least half of us joked we weren't sure we wanted them to stop the fight." Chloe laughs at the memory. "I know it's terrible to think that, but we were all so tired of Morley's abuse that for once, we couldn't help but enjoy watching someone give it back."

"What happened after that?"

"The CPPD came, and naturally, Morley pressed charges. The court granted Morley a restraining order, and Owen had to attend counseling."

I pound my fist on the table I'm so frustrated. "If Owen Munoz has a history of violence against Haynes, why aren't the cops looking at him?"

"I don't know," Chloe responds sadly.

"Do you know where we can find Mr. Munoz so I can talk to him?"

"I'm sorry, I don't. He's mostly been a recluse since his wife died. I'm surprised he came into your cafe. I only see him around town occasionally."

"Okay, I guess I'll have to figure out a way to find him tomorrow."

"As much as I appreciate your taking the time to listen to me about this, I believe you offered to feed me as well?" Chloe laughs.

"Oh, my goodness! I almost forgot about dinner!" I jump up and run to the kitchen.

"Can I do anything to help?" Chloe calls after me.

"Nope, it's all good. Just have a seat at the table, and I'll bring out some more wine."

In short order, Chloe and I are enjoying a dinner that's pure snowy evening comfort food. I made a simple yet exquisite tomato soup from a recipe Damien gave me. Just canned tomatoes, onion, butter, and vegetable stock.

Then we top it off with a side salad, and panini pressed gruyere cheese sandwiches. Also, thanks to a Damien recipe, I smear a bit of dijon mustard on whole grain bread and top them with caramelized sweet onions. I have the best friends. Miranda helps me with magic, and Damien helps me with cooking.

It's times like this that I realize how grateful I am for friends who have become my family, plus a boyfriend and familiars who, even though they love to try my patience, make me laugh and feel special.

Chapter 13

The next morning, on the drive into Marcall's, I'm surprised to see how much it snowed overnight. I love being the first person to touch fresh snow. The snowflakes sparkle in the lights from the street lamps, and the snow crunches under my car tires. You know it's early when the snowplows haven't been out yet.

The rabbits hop easily through the snow, but Stumpy insists I carry him into Marcall's because he doesn't like to get his stumps wet. At least, this is what the rabbits tell me. Sometimes I think if they wanted to, they could tell wild stories about the things Stumpy has supposedly told them, and I would be none the wiser. Hopefully, they never figure that out. Nonetheless, Stumpy seems quite happy about being carried into the cafe.

As promised, Aranya has already arrived, made the coffee, and is starting on the day's selections. I still haven't figured out how we'll track down Mr. Munoz to question him, but I'm hoping the answer will fall into my lap as it often does around here.

I'm shocked to find a few customers outside waiting for us to open at 6:30. I know our food is incredible, but I'm not sure that even I would wait in the snow for it. Gladys bustles in the door with the rest of them, but is horrified to learn that Damien is out for the day.

"But, but, who is making my burrito?" she sputters.

"Oh, no worries, Aranya has it covered," I reassure her as I point to Aranya through the window, and she waves back cheerfully.

"Are you sure she knows what she's doing?" Gladys asks in a stage whisper.

"Yes!" I respond in the same whisper. "She's very good, I promise."

"Hmmm. Okay." Gladys says, looking between the two of us like she doesn't believe a word I'm saying.

Aranya, knowing that Gladys likes her burrito just so and at just the right time, hurries out with it. Damien left explicit instructions on how Gladys' vegan burrito must be prepared and delivered within seconds of her coming in.

"Damien isn't sick, is he? Poor thing. Does he need some soup delivered? Does that husband of his even know how to cook? Damien shouldn't have to cook when he's ill."

"I swear to you, Damien isn't sick."

"Well then, where is he?"

I don't want to tell her why he's out today, without his permission. Especially since we don't know for sure if they'll get approved for fostering, even though I can't imagine they'll be turned down.

"You know what, Gladys? I can't tell you why Damien is out today. Not yet anyway. It's a personal matter."

"Hmmm," Gladys is still looking at me suspiciously. "I guess I'll have to take your word for it, for now. But you'd tell me if something was wrong, wouldn't you?"

"Yes, I swear I would tell you if something was wrong with Damien."

With that, Gladys digs into her burrito. Hopefully, I won't have to hold her off for very long. Given her penchant for sniffing out gossip, I suspect she may figure out what's going on before long.

Once the snowplow comes through town, and the roads are cleared, we do a brisk business all morning long. Crested Peaks townspeople are used to the snow anyway, so it's not a big deal for them. And with a lot of tourists staying at the Hotel Glacier, they just walk over.

I'm caught off guard, however, when Neil Doyle, Shauna's boyfriend, stops in mid-morning.

"Hey there Neil, welcome to Marcall's."

"Uh, hi," he responds.

I realize that even though I know exactly who he is; I don't think he remembers me from the other day as the missing shoe lady.

"Is Damien here?"

"No, he's out for the day. Can I help you with something?" I ask, thinking about how Damien seems extra popular around here today.

"My girlfriend and I are getting married, and we wanted to talk to him about catering our reception."

"Oh!" Shauna and Neil got engaged? When did this happen? "When did you get engaged?" I ask because this seems sudden. I have to think Shauna would have mentioned it the other day wouldn't she?

"Just yesterday," he answers.

"Oh yay! And congratulations."

"Should I just come back later, maybe? When Damien is here? I don't even know if he does catering, but we just love his cooking so much we thought we'd check."

"You know what? Why don't you leave your contact information, and I'll have him get back to you?"

Neil nods his head. "Sure, that will work, thanks."

I grab a piece of paper and pen from underneath the cash register and hand it to him while I watch him scribble down his information. Just as he's finishing up his note, he bumps a stack of clean dishes I have sitting on the counter, and they nearly fall to the floor. Luckily, I stop them all, freezing them in mid-air.

"I'm so sorry, that was a close call." He smiles when he realizes the plates are frozen in place. "You're a witch," he says.

"I'm not sure I'm a very good one," I explain as I reverse direction on the plates, but miss one that crashes to the floor.

"Oh my gosh, I'm such a klutz. Let me pay for that," he insists.

"Nonsense," I tell him. "I drop dishes all the time. I won't let you pay for it."

"How about I order two breakfast burritos to go, then? I'm starving, and as I already said, my fiance and I love Damien's cooking."

"Now that I'll let you do. What kind?"

"How about two Damien Specials?"

I poke my head through the window to tell Aranya that we need two specials, as we like to call them. Then I ring up Neil's purchase at the cash register while storing his note in a safe place for Damien to find when he gets back.

"Enjoy the burritos!" I call out as he leaves.

"I'm sure I will!" he responds.

He waves at us as he walks past the huge picture window in front, and I see him pass Drew on the sidewalk.

"Hey there stranger!" I say, happy to see my hardworking boyfriend pay us a visit.

"I'm just here to grab a burrito for lunch and ask you if you want to go to the North Pole Pop Up Sale tonight at the Evergreen Town Square to do some Christmas shopping."

"Oh, yeah, that would be fun! I'm in."

"Maybe we could grab a pizza afterward for dinner?" he offers, knowing the quickest way to curry favor with me is pizza.

"That sounds even better!" I tell him. "Can I ask how the case is going?" I don't need to tell him which one he obviously knows.

"I promise that we are investigating every angle, but you have to know that finding that syringe in Chloe's truck is still the most damning piece of evidence we have. Just because everybody in town despised Morley doesn't make them all viable suspects."

"I get it. I just—"

Drew holds up his hand. "I know, you just know that Chloe didn't do this. But that's not enough to ignore the murder weapon found on her property."

"But she told me that when she got there, the morning after Morley died, the door was unlocked, and she never leaves it unlocked."

"And she explained all of that to us as well. But if that's true, she should have contacted us immediately, rather than opening the truck for business and planning to call us later that day," Drew scolds.

"But how could she have known someone broke in and planted the syringe? She's being framed!"

"Or she made that up. We have no evidence that anyone other than Chloe had been in the truck. We only have her claim that the door was unlocked when she got there. Until we have something concrete on someone else, she remains our number one suspect."

I sigh heavily. Why does he always have to be so practical?

"Have you heard anything from Damien, by the way? I know the social worker was going to their home this morning."

"We haven't heard anything yet, but you're an even bigger hero to him than you already were, I hope you know!"

"Why?" Drew asks, looking genuinely confused.

"Because of your glowing recommendation! They told Damien that they nearly skipped the home visit based on your word alone."

"Oh, well, that's great." Drew says, blushing. "I'm happy to help. I'm sure he and Tom will be great foster parents. And I have to get back to work now," he declares, glancing at the clock. "But I'll see you after work," he tells me, leaning in to give me a quick kiss. I swear it's utterly crazy that after nearly a year of being with him, my stomach still flip flops every time we kiss.

As soon as he leaves, three more hungry customers come in, and after that, we have a steady flow of diners for the next hour. It just starts to slow down when I get a text:

Charlotte, this is Shauna. I need you at the travel agency immediately.

What on earth could be wrong? For a moment, I get my hopes up. She wants to confess to murdering her step dad. But of course, it's never that easy.

I write back. **What's up? Are you okay?**

Just get over here as fast as you can.

In the past, I've gotten in trouble with Drew for responding to texts like this without contacting him first. But as I start to press his number on the phone, I reconsider. It's just Shauna asking me to come to the travel agency and not meet behind the Hotel Glacier, like last time. And I'm pretty sure if I tell Drew that Shauna texted me and told me to come over right away, he's going to wonder why I'm bothering him with something so silly.

"Hey Aranya, are you okay by yourself for a bit? Shauna wants to see me at the travel agency."

"Really? Why is she asking for you? She just met you."

"I don't know," I shrug, "but I think it's worth seeing what she wants."

"Okay, sure, I'm fine here. If I get into trouble, I'll text you."

"Thanks, and make sure the rabbits and Stumpy stay here. I don't feel like chasing them down when we close tonight."

"Will do, boss!"

I throw on a coat and walk quickly toward the travel agency. The wind is particularly biting today, and I don't want to be out in the cold weather for long. I slow down though, when I see a CPPD patrol car parked out front. Great. What's going on now?

I almost turn back when I realize if Drew finds out I'm here, and thinks I'm interfering in their investigation, he'll be fired up. But then the cold air spurs me on. I'm sure it's nothing. Maybe the officers who were driving the car aren't even in the travel agency. They could be next door, at the Roses are Red Flower Shop, right?

But when I get closer, I see that the CPPD is indeed inside the travel agency talking to Shauna, and it's Drew with a patrol officer. I start to turn on my heel, hoping no one saw me when Shauna spots me and waves frantically at me to come in.

Drew turns around to see who she's waving at and when he realizes it's me, he doesn't look happy. As usual, I'll have to plead innocence and tell him I didn't come down here on purpose and that Shauna texted me.

"Hey, what's up?" I ask, trying to sound nonchalant.

"Oh Charlotte, I'm so glad you're here. I didn't know who else to call!"

"You called us!" the patrolman points out.

"I mean besides you," she says, like that was the silliest thing she ever heard.

"You said it was urgent?" I ask, shrugging my shoulders at Drew, who's really giving me the stink eye now.

I have proof. I can show him the texts!

"Someone broke in here while I was at lunch and left this on my desk!" Shauna wails, snatching a piece of paper from the patrolman's hands.

Now he's the one glaring at me.

She shoves the paper in my face. The message appears to be written with a black sharpie in big letters: **You're next!** And then a picture of what I assume is meant to be a cupcake. She looks really scared.

"Did Chloe do this?" she suggests. "I heard she's out on bail."

"Uhhhhh," is all I can think of to say right that second. But then a resounding, "No! There's no way."

"That's evidence!" Drew growls while holding his hand out. I gingerly place the note back in his hands. The officer with him holds up a large plastic bag that they place the note in.

"Do you have any security cameras in here?" Drew asks.

"Yes, of course," Shauna responds.

"We'll need to see the footage," the officer says as he scans the ceiling for the cameras.

"No problem, I'll transfer this afternoon's footage to a flashdrive, and you can take it with you." Shauna puts her hand on Drew's wrist, and I notice it's trembling. "Do you honestly think I'm in danger? I can't imagine that anyone who knew me at all would think I supported Morley in any way."

Then she touches *my* arm. "Charlotte, can you remind Chloe that I hated Morley and I'm glad she killed him? I think she did us all a favor. I don't understand why she would turn to me next!"

"Charlotte will do no such thing," Drew responds so sharply that Shauna and I both jump. "She's not supposed to be involved in any case, although clearly she's been here recently. Officer Morgan here will discuss this with Chloe, not Charlotte."

"I understand," Shauna whispers. "Whatever you think is best."

"No way Chloe did this Shauna, it has to be the real killer." I squeeze in before Drew can kick me out of here.

He turns to me. "Charlotte, you can go back to work now. And do not contact Chloe!"

I nod my head as I scamper out the door. I just don't know what to say to Shauna. I can't imagine Chloe doing something like this, which means there's still a killer out there, and I'm worried who could be next.

I walk as quickly as I can back to Marcall's. Since I'm not supposed to tell Chloe about this, I need to talk this over with Miranda. She's sure to have answers. I duck into Marcall's first though to make sure Aranya is still okay before heading across the street. But when I open the door, Miranda pounces. I swear she has radar.

"Have you heard anything from Damien?" Miranda asks.

"I was just getting ready to come talk to you!" I blurt out.

"Oh no, it's bad news!"

"How did you know?" I ask.

"I didn't, really. I'm just guessing."

"Wait, what are you talking about?"

"What are *you* talking about?" Miranda asks, raising an eyebrow at me.

Aranya shakes her head. "You're talking about two different things. Miranda is wondering if you've heard from Damien about the social worker's visit."

"Oh." I pause. "I haven't, and it's making me really anxious. What if something went wrong?"

"Or maybe no news is good news?"

"I don't know, but I really want to text him and find out what's going on. Maybe he doesn't know yet? Or may they already told him they didn't pass?"

"How could they not pass?" Miranda looks skeptical. "There's no way, right? They must be a shoo-in."

As we continue to debate whether to reach out to Damien to find out what's happened, we don't even realize he's walked in the door.

"Ahem."

We turn around. "Damien!" I shout.

"How did it go?" Miranda cries. "Are you parents? Did you pass? Do you have your little girl yet? What happened? We need to know!" she blusters, grabbing him by the shoulders and nearly shaking him into submission. She really needs to stop sampling so much of her own supply.

Damien grabs Miranda's hands to keep from falling over backward. "We passed!"

"No way! That's amazing!" I exclaim.

Breathing a tremendous sigh of relief, he turns to me. "We owe Drew big time. He really put us over the finish line. The social worker said Drew's recommendation was huge."

"Wow!" Miranda says, her eyes shimmering with happy tears.

"So what's next? Are you still getting the little girl?"

"She should move in by this weekend. But now we need to shop for furniture! We need a bed, and a dresser, and a nightlight, and I think we also need a little table for arts and crafts or reading or whatever she wants to do, and she'll need toys and clothes. I can't believe this is happening!"

By now, Damien seems on the verge of hyperventilating, so I steer him over to a chair to sit down and relax. I don't need him passing out in the middle of the cafe.

"There's plenty of time for that," I reassure him.

"I'm happy to fill in for you as long as you need!" Aranya shouts from the back.

"See, we've got you covered. You'll be fine."

"Okay, yeah, of course, I'm just so excited I can't believe it. I should go back. I just wanted to tell you guys the good news in person. A text just didn't seem right given the circumstances."

"Either way, I'm glad you let us know. We were getting worried," I tell him, patting him on the back. "You guys will make fabulous parents. She is so lucky to have found you."

"Hang on a second," Miranda says, finally remembering and turning to me. "Where were you earlier, and why did you say you had bad news for me?"

"Why do you have bad news?" Damien asks.

"You know, it's not important right now. We'll talk about it later. Right now, we're just here to celebrate. Just stay five more minutes," I insist. "I think I saw some champagne in the refrigerator once upon a time—"

"Got it!" Aranya shouts, brandishing the bottle I knew Damien must have stashed in there, just in case.

"Grab some glasses and bring it out!" I tell her as I flip the sign outside to close and lock the door. It's almost closing time anyway, and we need something to celebrate.

Chapter 14

After we all enjoy a glass of champagne, I send everyone home for the evening, and then Drew shows up for our pop-up shopping trip. They plowed the entire town square while installing heat lamps around the area to melt the snow and keep shoppers warm. Directly in the center of the town square is an enchanted ice rink. Not just the fake ice like they show on tv but an actual frozen pond that will be available until Valentine's Day.

Shop keepers have packed away the Halloween decorations for the year and hung up Christmas decorations in their place. Lights twinkle, garland sparkles, and holiday music plays in the background, hoping no doubt to get shoppers in a mood to spend money. The scents of hot chocolate, funnel cakes, and roasting chestnuts make me want to run from booth to booth and grab at least one of everything.

Even though we tried to sneak out while the three boys were sleeping, they chased after us at the last minute. Then they convinced me to take them in the wagon, which they then also insisted I bewitch with colorful and festive lights. They point out that if I just let them run loose, I'll end up chasing them all evening to get them back to the cafe, but if I wheel them around in the wagon, I'll know exactly where they are. The three of them know exactly how to work me.

The Five Dachshund Bakery has a booth, but my efforts to sneak by are met with howls of protest. Stumpy is meowing like he hasn't eaten in days, which causes many shoppers to stop and stare. Like they weren't already staring at the three of them being towed in a bright red Radio Flyer steel wagon leftover from my childhood.

The rabbits openly boo me, which thankfully no one else can hear. But when they realize that, they stomp their feet against the steel bottom, which echoes all over the shopping area. I end up buying more than enough treats for all three. When I insist they're for Christmas presents only, they threaten to start up again. But when I tell them I'm returning the treats, they stop. For now, at least.

I pick out a handmade wooden pepper mill for Aranya with swirling natural wood colors and hand rubbed with clear finish. The artist who created it said that no two were exactly alike.

For Damien, I get a new apron that reads "Best Dad Ever" and a matching apron for Poppy that reads "Dad's Sous Chef."

I select a chocolate lover's dream box for Miranda that's so pretty they may not last until Christmas in my hands. It has chocolate covered sea salt caramels, hand crafted dark chocolate truffles that are so pretty they look more like art than food, and hot chocolate bombs made of chocolate on the outside, stuffed with chocolate chips and marshmallows on the inside.

"Any updates on the note left at the travel agency?" I ask Damien.

"Our forensic handwriting analyzer said that it was almost certainly written by a left-handed individual," Drew explains.

"That's it?"

"It's the best we have so far. And given that only a small percentage of the population is left-handed, it might help somewhat."

I stop in my tracks.

"What is it?" Drew asks.

"Chloe is left-handed," I whisper, which I immediately regret disclosing.

I feel better though, when Drew admits they already knew that. Not better that Chloe is left-handed, but better that I didn't admit anything they didn't already know.

But when I spot Owen Munoz just mere feet away, I think I'm imagining it for a moment. When I realize it's him for sure, I grab Drew's arm. "Drew! Look!" I point in the distance.

"What are we looking at?"

"That's Owen Munoz! I've been wracking my brain trying to figure out how to find him!"

"And why are you looking for Mr. Munoz?" he asks, giving me one of those intense stares that I've become all too familiar with.

"Errrrr."

"Never mind, I already know. And believe it or not, we've been trying to track him down too."

"Are you kidding? Why?"

"When we searched Morley's house after the murder, we found a box full of threatening emails and letters."

"There were so many people who despised Morley that he kept copies of their threats?" I ask.

"Yep!" he says.

"And Owen Munoz has been one of his loudest critics. Did you know Morley even took out a restraining order against him?"

"I'm aware of that. Do I even want to know how you know that?" he asks.

I wiggle my hand back and forth to indicate it's debatable. "Remember, he was in Marcall's the day after Morley died, and when he saw the article in the newspaper about Morley's death, he was thrilled. Like, dance a jig happy."

"Let's go talk to him. Hopefully, with you at my side and the fact we're not in a police station, he'll be a little more inclined to open up."

"Wait just a minute. Does this mean I get to accompany you to question a suspect?"

Drew sighs. I can tell this is painful for him. "I suppose," he groans.

"Yeeee!" I exclaim, clapping my hands. Okay, so maybe that was a bit over the top, but I feel like a six-year-old getting a new bike.

"Just play it cool, wouldja?" he insists.

"Okay, got it, super cool."

"Mr. Munoz, hello!" Drew calls out as we approach him. "Detective Andrew Bailey from the CPPD, we've been trying to reach you."

"I don't really enjoy talking to cops," he says as he starts to turn away, but then stops when he sees me.

"Well, hello there. Charlotte, right?"

"Yes, Mr. Munoz, nice to see you again!"

"I keep thinking about that fabulous meal I had at your cafe and I need to get back again very soon."

"You absolutely should!" I tell him as I feel Drew poking me in the back, encouraging me to keep talking.

"I keep thinking about how when you were in Marcall's you mentioned that you were glad Morley died after you saw the article in the newspaper, I mean."

"You're darn right I am. That guy was a worthless piece of garbage, and we're all better off with him dead."

"That must have been a heartbreaking experience for you, aside from losing your wife, I mean."

"I still have nightmares about it."

"Mr. Munoz," Drew breaks in. "We're well aware of your history with Mr. Haynes. And when we searched his house after he died, we found a lot of letters from you threatening to harm him. In addition to the restraining order he took out against you. Can you tell us where you were on Halloween night?"

Owen takes a deep breath and looks somewhat embarrassed. "Am I a suspect?"

"If you could just answer the question, we could rule you out as one right now."

"I admit, at one point, I truly wanted to beat that man senseless, to say the least. I used to fantasize about running into him in a dark alley somewhere, with a baseball bat, and just bash the living daylights out of him."

Gulp. I move a bit closer to Drew. This is making me so uncomfortable.

"But, when the court mandated I get therapy, it was the best thing that could have happened to me. I was able to talk through what happened, and I no longer feel compelled to physically harm him - even if I do plan to dance on his grave once he's buried."

"Were you at the Halloween Festival, Mr. Munoz?" I ask.

"You're still wondering if I killed him?"

"It occurred to me that you may have. And who could blame you, right?" I just realized we're doing good cop, bad cop, and I'm struggling not to show how excited I am about it.

"No, I wasn't at the Hotel Glacier on Halloween. I still don't go to parties like that. My dear wife, rest her soul, was the one who enjoyed those types of gatherings. And no, I didn't kill him. But when you figure out who did, let me know so I can shake their hand."

"If you weren't at the hotel party, where were you?"

"I was at home watching tv, I passed candy out to a few trick or treaters, and then I went to bed."

"Can anyone corroborate that, Mr. Munoz?" Drew asks.

He shrugs. "I guess the kids who got candy from me. Say, do you serve pancakes at your establishment?" he asks, turning to me.

"Uh, yes, we sure do!"

"I think I should stop in for some pancakes soon."

"I would love that."

"See you folks later," he says as he nods his head and turns and walks away.

I turn to Drew. "Do you believe him?"

"Not as a matter of practice. People can tell me all sorts of things, but I'm inclined not to believe them until I see proof. Or at the very least, I'm reserving judgment until I know more."

"He certainly isn't shy about his feelings regarding Morley. And I guess I don't blame him. That must have been so traumatic."

"I agree, but it's no excuse to kill someone."

"Does this mean you believe me when I tell you Chloe couldn't have done this?" I ask hopefully.

"It means I'm investigating all credible angles of this case. Chloe is still the one we have the most evidence to support as the murderer."

He can be such a party pooper when he wants to be. "I appreciate that you're at least investigating other possibilities," I tell him, thinking I should at least be gracious and thank him for not solely focusing on Chloe.

"Should we get a present for Tom and Damien's foster daughter?" Drew asks, surprising me once again. I find his stoic alpha male personality both sexy and exasperating at times. But then he asks if we should get a present for a little girl we haven't even met yet, and it makes me feel all warm and fuzzy.

"We should," I respond.

"I'm not really sure what little girls like. How old is she again?"

"She's three. And I bet she likes unicorns. I'm pretty sure every little girl likes unicorns. It's a rule or something."

We scour the pop-up market for unicorns when we come across a plush and colorful unicorn blanket that should be perfect for a cold Crested Peaks winter. "What do you think of this?" Drew asks, holding it up for me to see.

"I think she'll love it!"

On the way back to Marcall's, we stop at my car to pack some of the gifts in the trunk, when I spot a flier under the windshield wipers.

"Huh, what's this?" I mutter as I pull it from the windshield. "Oh no!" I exclaim. "Drew!" I say as I shove the piece of paper at him.

Back off!

The flier looks like it's written with the same print and sharpie that was left at the travel agency for Shauna.

Drew isn't happy at all. "Stay here," he tells me, "while I call this into the station. I want a team out here to look over the car and the cafe."

"Do you think they did something to Marcall's?" Now I'm terrified. What if they've vandalized my beloved cafe? And what if I had left the rabbits and Stumpy there while we were out shopping? I turn to run towards Marcall's, but Drew, anticipating exactly what I planned to do, grabs my arm.

"You are not to go anywhere near there until my team can go over everything and make sure it's safe."

"But-" I whimper.

"No buts! This is precisely why I don't like it when you nose around in police work, Char. We're dealing with criminals here. In this case, a murderer. Don't take another step until my guys get here."

"Okay," I agree reluctantly, while it takes every ounce of self-control I've got - which admittedly isn't much - to keep from running to my restaurant. But Drew is too fast, and I'll never make it there in time to check everything over, anyway.

I'll just have to wait until his people get here. Or until he turns his back. Unfortunately, he knows me so well he doesn't take his eyes off me until the squad car pulls up next to us.

Drew approaches the two patrolmen while one of them places the note in an evidence bag. He gestures at Marcall's, so one of them walks cautiously toward my restaurant. My heart is racing so hard it feels like a car engine revving.

After inspecting the front door, he signals that it's locked. That's somewhat of a relief, although they still need to check out the back door and ensure no one tampered with it, either. I recall my conversation with Chloe, where she said she found the door to her cupcake truck unlocked. The next thing she knew, she was being arrested for murder.

The other officer heads around back but radios us to tell us that door is still locked as well. Drew insists I unlock it with magic, so I don't have an excuse to go over there myself and potentially contaminate a crime scene. I unlock both doors, and the officers enter my cafe.

I can't help but recall when I found my original landlord's body in the alley after first moving here. And then I discovered Tony, the owner of the restaurant next door, stabbed to death. It gives me chills that are far deeper than the freezing cold air outside, and I rub my arms for comfort.

I know in reality it's only several minutes later, but it feels more like hours when the officers radio Drew to tell him it doesn't look as if anyone was in the restaurant while we were gone. When Drew gives me the go-ahead, I sprint for Marcalls, bursting in through the front door as I try to catch my breath from the adrenalin rush.

I have to see for myself everything is okay. Thankfully, it's all just as I left it a couple of hours ago. Nothing looks touched, and given that both doors were locked, I feel better. But I'm still nervous that someone knows I'm looking into this - I assume that someone is the killer - and wants me to back off.

And then I go from nervous to mad. You bet I'm investigating this. Someone in Crested Peaks is a killer, and they don't care if an innocent person goes to jail instead, and I won't stand for it.

Seeing the concern on my face, Drew tells me, "I've arranged to have a patrol car drive by your house every hour tonight just to be on the safe side. Given that whoever it was just left this on your car, but didn't touch your restaurant, it makes me think they're just trying to scare you. But I want you to be extra cautious right now. And I really need you to stay out of this. Let me and the CPPD handle this from now on, got it?"

I nod my head numbly. I can't believe this is happening, and while part of me is scared, the other part is more determined than ever to figure out who really killed Morley. But maybe we'll just keep that other part a secret from Drew.

Drew insists that we still get a pizza like we originally planned and then drive back to my house. The three boys are in the back seat and the rabbits chatter on non-stop about the note. "I swear if someone tries to break into our house, I'll bite them right on the ankle!" I hear Marshall telling the other two.

"I'll bite them on the other ankle!" Marcus offers.

I can only imagine what Stumpy must be thinking as they talk. "Stumpy says he would scratch their eyes out, in case you were wondering," Marshall informs me.

I feed the rabbits and Stumpy their dinner while Drew gets out some plates and the wine for our dinner. We plop down in front of the fireplace to eat and I admit I'm exhausted. It's been a crazy day, full of ups and downs.

"Did you know that Morley didn't approve of Supernaturals and Non Supernaturals dating?" I ask Drew.

"Where did you hear that?" he responds. "Not that I'm surprised or anything. That guy was the worst. Everyone we've talked to has pointed out how glad they are he's gone."

I refrain from telling him I've had the same experience since I'm not supposed to be in the middle of this. "Shauna told me. But then Neil stopped by the cafe and asked if Damien could cater their wedding reception because they just got engaged. And Chloe said that Morley had control of Shauna's trust. Hey, you haven't found that in Morley's things, have you?"

"A copy of the trust?" Drew asks. "No, but we've been looking for that and Morley's will."

We both fall silent as we take another bite of pizza. Police work is not only tiring, it makes me hungry.

"Is there any way to confirm Mr. Munoz alibi?"

Drew shakes his head. "Probably not. Not unless one of his neighbors can tell us they specifically saw him at home passing out candy."

I don't think Drew is aware yet that we talked to Ethan Davis, and if he knew we made up this complicated ruse to get to him, I'm sure he'd be mad. And as much as I don't want to get myself in trouble, I really don't want to get Damien in trouble now that they've been approved as foster parents.

"I never even asked Chloe where she was when Morley was killed." I suddenly remember.

"She was at the hotel, overseeing the cupcake display," Drew says matter-of-factly.

"Oh." I gulp. "Police work is hard."

Drew laughs. "No kidding!"

Chapter 15

Thankfully, it was a quiet night, and I got some sleep. I felt safer knowing a patrol car was driving by on a regular basis, and this morning, when I peer out the front window, there's one parked in front of my house. I quickly magic some coffee for them and take it outside.

Then I load the boys into the car and head for work with the patrol car following. After parking in the lot, the officers follow me into Marcall's, where Damien is back at work and already preparing for the day as usual.

"Whoa, what the..." he sputters when he sees me walk in with not just the usual two rabbits and a cat, but a police officer as well.

"It's just a precaution," I tell him. "They aren't staying or anything, right?" I ask.

"Just making sure everything is on the up and up," the officer replies.

When I explain the note I found on my car yesterday, and the message they found at the travel agency, Damien starts in right away in full dad mode. They don't even have a kid yet, and he's got this thing down pat. "How many times have I warned you to be careful, boss?"

"Don't freak out on me. It's all good. Drew thinks they were just trying to scare me and that I'm not in any real danger."

"As evidenced by your police escort," he says sarcastically.

"They just followed me to work this morning," I explain, as if that's better.

"You mean they were at your house last night?" he howls as he gets louder and more high-pitched.

"They weren't *at* my house all night," I tell him as I motion with my hands for him to calm down. "They were just driving by regularly to make sure everything was okay."

"Do they have any suspects yet?"

"They know a left-handed person wrote the notes."

He waves a wooden spoon to punctuate his words. "You realize you're not making this any better, right?"

"Are you guys all ready for Poppy to move in?" I ask, hoping to change the subject and distract him.

"Slick move, trying to distract me," he points out.

"Did it work?" I ask.

"Now that you mention it, I have a dilemma," he tells me.

"And what is that?"

"I have to find a little girl's unicorn bed."

"That's what the internet is for, right? Hey, did you say unicorn?"

"Yes, Poppy loves unicorns. More than you can imagine, loves unicorns."

"Ha!" I exclaim. I knew it. Little girls love unicorns.

"Okay, well, here's the thing. When she lived with her mom, apparently she had a pink unicorn bed." He shows me a picture, and it's bright pink. We're talking obnoxiously bright pink. The headboard has a unicorn, and a rainbow painted on it, and then at the foot of the bed, which is still blindingly pink, there's a huge glittering heart. "After her mom died, and she went into foster care, she obviously couldn't take the bed with her. And when we agreed to foster her, DHHS tried to get the bed back, but it's long gone, and they don't know where it went. And she has been crying over this bed. Has already started writing letters to Santa for a new matching bed."

"Oh, that breaks my heart. She lost everything, and now all she wants is a piece of her home." Tears swim in my eyes. I know exactly how she feels. At least I was a little older when I lost my parents. How do you tell a three-year-old her mom is never coming home? The least she could have is a bed she loves.

"I have looked everywhere and called every furniture store from here to Colorado Springs, and no one has a bed even remotely like this."

"Could someone custom make one for you?"

"With the holidays, they're all backed up with orders from now until Valentine's Day, and I really wanted her to have this bed when she arrived."

"That's awful. What are you going to do?"

"I guess I'll have to just find the best one I can. Maybe a princess bed or something?"

"I would think you could find a pink princess bed somewhere."

"Yeah, time is running short. She's supposed to be here Sunday evening, so we obviously need something for her!"

"I really hope you find something in time. She's already been through so much at such a young age."

"I'll just have to keep looking. If I find a place in Denver, is it okay to skip out and go get it?"

"But of course!" I tell him. "Oh, and when you were out yesterday, Neil Doyle stopped by looking for you."

"Shauna's boyfriend?" he asks.

"Now fiance," I tell him as I hand him the note he left.

"They want me to cater their wedding reception, huh? I've never done anything like that."

"Give him a call and see what he wants you to do. He said they both love your cooking."

Damien shrugs. "I had no idea but I guess I'll look into it."

"Hey, what time do you think the mortuary opens today?"

"No."

"No, what?"

"You know very well missy."

Wow, he really is getting to be a dad.

"Drew told me yesterday that they found a box of threatening letters in Morley's house after he died, and that Owen Munoz and Ethan Davis wrote most of them. I just want to have another conversation with Ethan, that's all. No biggie."

"You do still realize how bad this all sounds, right? You just keep talking and talking like you're going to say something to convince me none of this is a big deal. But it's not working! You need to just stay here today and let the CPPD handle it all." He pauses like he expects me to agree with him or something. "What are you doing on your phone?"

"I'm looking to see when the mortuary opens."

Damien smacks himself on the forehead and turns back to stirring the pot of black beans, cursing in Spanish as he often does when I make him crazy.

"You know you're going to have to watch your language around your foster daughter, right?"

"How will she know what I'm saying in the first place?"

"You said she's from Puerto Rico, right? How do you know her mother didn't teach her Spanish?"

I laugh when he pauses mid stir. Ha! Got him.

He returns to stirring while looking at me sideways, but I notice he's no longer cursing, just pinching his lips together as if he's trying desperately not to say anything further.

The mortuary opens at 9 AM, which is awfully convenient because that's when Aranya comes in today, too, so I won't have to leave Damien in the cafe alone. As soon as she arrives, I let her know where I'm going and then dash out the door, much to Damien's chagrin.

▢▢▢▢▢▢

When I step up to the front desk, I see a bright orange sign that wasn't there when we were here last time. "Welcome! We are now part of the Kamfield Family."

What the heck is that? I point to the sign and ask the receptionist. "What is this?"

"Oh, Mr. Haynes sold the mortuary to the Kamfield Corporation before he died."

"I still don't know what Kamfield is."

"It's a national chain of mortuaries."

"But I thought Ethan was being groomed to take over. He's still in charge, right?"

Now it's the receptionist's turn to look confused. "Oh no, he's gone."

"Gone on vacation or gone, gone. Like never coming back."

"He's gone gone," she says simply.

"A sale like this couldn't just happen overnight. He had to have planned for this before he died, yes?"

She nods her head, "Oh yeah."

This poor woman must think I'm the most annoying person in the world, or at least the weirdest, because I keep asking her all these questions. "So did Ethan know that Mr. Haynes sold to Kamfield before he died?"

"Of course he did. We all did. They called us in for a meeting months ago, and he told us he was selling. A lot of the smaller mortuaries are doing it now. It's too expensive to maintain an independent mortuary long term, and so the corporate chains are offering big bucks to take over established businesses."

"So if Ethan knew, why did he keep coming back to work and claiming that he was getting ready to take over?"

"I'm afraid you'll have to ask him that. I kind of need to get back to my customers. Do you need to schedule a funeral or did you just come in to ask about Ethan?"

I turn back to see several people waiting impatiently for me to finish grilling the receptionist.

"Sorry about that, have a nice day."

"Next!" she proclaims.

I wander out of the mortuary. Ethan knew that Morley was selling to Kamfield and that he was out. That definitely gives him a reason to kill Morley. Add to that the evidence that Drew has with proof of him threatening Morley all the time.

As I walk up the sidewalk trying to figure out what just happened, I'm so lost in thought it takes me a while to register that I'm being followed. My pulse races as I chide myself for going to the mortuary alone to begin with. Why didn't I listen to Drew and Damien for once?

Whoever it is, I'm not going down without a fight. I'll run, I'll kick, I'll scratch, I'll use whatever magic I can think of - it's worked every other time after all - to take them down. I pause, waiting for the footsteps to get closer. Let them think I've given up.

When I spin around and come face to face with Drew, I scream. Then I feel like a dope. "Drew! What on earth? You scared me to death! I thought I was being followed by the killer."

Drew puts his hands on his hips and glares at me silently.

"You were following me on purpose, weren't you? That little fink Damien called you, didn't he? Ohhh wait til I see him."

"Damien didn't say a word. I told the patrol car to watch the cafe today. When the officers saw you leave and go to the mortuary, they called me."

"Oh." Oops.

"What were you doing at the mortuary? As if I didn't already know."

"I wanted to talk to Ethan."

"I'm shocked."

"Sarcasm doesn't become you, you know."

"And getting injured, or worse, by someone who has already killed one person, and threatened two others, doesn't become *you*."

"It doesn't really matter at this point because he wasn't there anyway," I explain.

"Where is he?"

"He got fired."

Drew looks confused. "Rumor has it that he got fired all the time but came back, anyway."

"That was when Morley was in charge."

"Obviously, Morley isn't in charge anymore, but Ethan told the CPPD he was on track to take over as General Manager before Haynes died."

"That's the story he was telling everyone, but it turns out Morley had already sold the mortuary to Kamfield, a corporate mortuary chain."

Drew rubs his hand over his chin, as he often does when he's pondering something. I notice he hasn't shaved for several days again. He's been so wrapped up in this case. "This is a twist."

"Isn't it, though?"

"Supposedly, Morley promised that he was grooming Ethan to take over when he retired. So Ethan tolerates his abuse all this time, thinking he would eventually take over, leaving Morley to retire somewhere far away. But now, all of that is for naught because a big corporate chain owns it. Talk about adding insult to injury."

"Add to that all the times Ethan threatened him before any of this happened," I point out.

"Right. I think we should pay Mr. Davis a visit at his home."

I gasp. "We? As in you and me, or you mean one of your officers?"

"I mean you and me believe it or not. You did give me the tip that the mortuary was sold. Even though you weren't supposed to be there in the first place."

"Goody!" I exclaim.

"But you do everything exactly as I tell you to. No matter what. And keep in mind this doesn't make you a police detective by any stretch of the imagination."

"Whatever you say, detective!" I tell him, giving him a smart salute.

We get into Drew's car and drive over to Ethan's house. I'm hoping he's home, and this isn't all a waste. Besides, what a bummer that the one time Drew lets me accompany him on official business is all for nothing if he isn't there. There's a car parked in the driveway, so I hope that means we're in luck.

As Drew knocks on the door, I cross all the fingers and toes I can that he answers. "Ethan Davis! Crested Peaks Police! Open up!"

The door cracks open just a bit, and one eye peeps out at us.

"Mr. Davis, Detective Bailey with the CPPD, may we have a word with you?" Drew asks.

I'm embarrassed to admit it, but this is so exciting.

"I already told the police everything I know."

"I understand that, but we have a few follow-up questions if you don't mind."

"Okay," he sighs as he opens the door reluctantly.

I'm praying he won't recognize me from the other day. He must come across dozens of people a day. I'm sure he won't remember a tall lady with long pink hair, right?

He points at me. "Hey, don't I know you?"

Drew turns and looks at me questioningly.

"I don't think so," I mumble. Big mistake.

"Wait! Yes! Of course! You came in with your husband looking to pre-purchase burial plots! I'm so sorry, but I can't help you anymore. I've been let go from the mortuary."

Oh man, is my face red. Drew will have a fit over this.

"So you've already met my colleague, Charlotte Duffin? And her *husband,* I guess?"

"Yes, a lovely couple they are. They're so cute together, don't you think?" he asks.

Tagging along with Drew on official business isn't so fun anymore. I wonder what the chances are of a sinkhole suddenly occurring right where I'm standing?

"They're as cute as can be," Drew growls. "Anyway," he says, while still glaring at me, "the first time we spoke you admitted to arguing with Mr. Morley Haynes, at the Hotel Glacier, shortly before he was killed. You also told us he fired you that night, but you just took it as one of his usual firings."

"Yes, that's right." Ethan nods his head. "Morley did that all the time, so I figured it was just a matter of time before he came around and let me come back to work."

Then I butt in. "But we just came from the mortuary where the receptionist told us not only had Morley sold the mortuary to Kamfield, you knew about it and knew you'd never become General Manager." Police work is a lot more fun when I'm not the one getting caught in a lie.

Ethan's shoulders slump. "Okay, you're right. All this time, I thought if I just kept coming back to work, I'd eventually become the manager. And then that piece of trash sells the entire place to a chain. I couldn't believe it."

"Is that what you were arguing about on Halloween at the hotel?" Drew asks.

"Yes," Ethan sighs.

"Can you tell us where you went after you argued with Mr. Haynes?" Drew asks.

"But I already told you that. I told you I picked up some takeout and then went straight home," he protests.

"Can anyone corroborate your alibi?"

"I don't think so," he responds.

"Do you have a receipt for the takeout?"

Drew is getting tough!

"Um, I must have one somewhere around here," Ethan mumbles while beginning to sweat.

"So if you picked up dinner and then came home right after the argument with Morley, can you explain why his home security cameras caught you vandalizing his garage door that night by spray painting this, uh, design?" Drew says, brandishing his iPad to show Ethan the footage. Whoa. What is this?

The color drains from Ethan's face as he watches video of himself spray painting Morley's garage door with an obscene gesture one normally makes with one's middle finger. Well played Detective McHotty! It's almost hard not to laugh at the clip of Ethan attempting to spray paint his clumsy artwork onto Morley's garage door. Although if he's the killer, I guess it's no laughing matter.

"All right, I admit it. I didn't go straight home after the party. I went to Morley's house first. I was just so angry. You have to understand."

"Sure, I understand. I have another follow up question though."

Ethan nods his head. If this guy doesn't pass out from the stress, I'll be shocked.

"One of the Hotel Glacier employees admitted to seeing you 'sneaking around the kitchen' were his words, after your very public argument with Haynes, and right before he was killed. Can you explain that?"

Ethan goes from pail to slightly green and I stare at Drew in shock. He obviously didn't tell me he knew that. Ethan could have snuck into the kitchen, poisoned Morley's cupcake and left!

"Do I need a lawyer?" he asks.

"I don't know, do you?" Drew responds.

"I swear to you I didn't kill Morley. Even though I lied about all the other stuff. It's just because I knew how bad it would look, that's all."

"Were you in the kitchen after you argued with Morley?"

Ethan shakes his head, and I'm convinced he's going to insist he talk to his lawyer before he says another word to us. Why wouldn't he? He's in serious trouble here. Maybe Drew will arrest him and then we'll have to drive to the police station together. This is getting exciting again.

"Okay, I admit it," he moans, holding his hands up.

I can't believe I'm about to hear a murderous confession, and Chloe will go free.

"I was in the kitchen because Pete was selling me some brownies."

"Brownies?" I shriek. "Who lies about buying brownies?" He's confessing to buying baked goods? What's wrong with him? Like anybody is going to believe that. I'm practically bouncing on my toes, waiting for Drew to slap the cuffs on him. Brownies. What an idiot.

"I'm pretty sure he means pot brownies," Drew says, rolling his eyes at me.

"But pot is legal," I point out. "You can get *'brownies'*," I say with air quotes and as much sarcasm as I can muster, "in any pot shop in Colorado. Why would you secretly buy brownies from someone when you don't need to?" I ask. Now I'm mad. Here I thought Chloe would be exonerated in just seconds, and this guy is supposedly lying about where he gets his pot?

"Do you know what edibles cost at the pot shop?" Ethan asks.

"Uh, no," I admit.

"They're expensive and when you add on the sales tax..." he says, shaking his head sorrowfully, "It may be legal, but it isn't cheap. Pete grows pot in his house, which is *legal*," he points out to Drew, "and then makes brownies that he sells to some of us on the side."

"That part isn't legal," Drew points out, "and that's why you have to sneak around to do it."

Now Ethan looks scared. I'm just happy he's about to go down for murder. I don't even care about his secret pot brownies, but whatever it takes.

"I need you to stay in town for the foreseeable future," Drew says.

I stare at Drew in disbelief. How are we not arresting this guy already?

"Yes, sir," Ethan whispers as he stares at the floor.

Just as we're about to leave, I can't help but notice a unique piece of art prominently displayed near the front window. It's so interesting looking I have to stop and stare. It's a bronze bust of a boy holding a kite, but is dark with an almost blue tint in places. "This is an amazing statue," I tell him.

"Believe it or not, I made that myself," Ethan says proudly.

"Did you really?"

"I was an art major before I got into business, so I love making things like this. Now that I've been fired for good this time, maybe I should go back to creating sculptures."

"You could sell them in town at Lucinda's Arts," I tell him.

He nods his head. "Thanks, I'll look into it."

"What was that all about?" Drew asks.

"Just admiring his sculpture," I try to convince him.

"Please, I know you, and I know when you're up to something. We're questioning a suspect, and all of a sudden you're advising him on a new art career."

"Okay, I was going to tell you more once we got in the car. But I happen to know that the bluish tint on the copper sculpture probably came from cyanide."

"You're kidding me. And where on earth did you learn that?" he asks.

"Remember, I lived in New York City before returning to Crested Peaks. My old boss had a thing for pricey, obnoxious art and copper sculptures. Mostly of naked women, those were his favorite."

Drew looks impressed. "Well, okay then, good to know."

"Don't you see what this means? If Ethan is making sculptures like that, he had access to cyanide! He could have easily used it to poison Morley. I don't understand why you haven't arrested him already!"

"I plan to look into everything we learned today, but that doesn't mean I can just arrest him on the spot. So far, this is all still just circumstantial."

"Fine, but I'm telling you, I'm sure Ethan is the one who killed Morley," I insist.

"And I'm not saying he didn't. I just need more evidence. I know one thing I can tell you for certain," he turns to me like he's about to announce some dramatic idea.

"What's that?

"I have a sudden craving for a breakfast burrito," Drew says as he opens the car door for me.

"And I know just where you can get one!" I laugh.

Chapter 16

"Hey, what happ-" Damien starts to ask when he sees me walk into the cafe but stops short when he sees Drew with me. "Uh oh."

"Uh oh is right," Drews tells him.

"I told her not to go," he says, looking at Drew. "But I didn't snitch!" he then exclaims, turning to me.

I hold my hand up. "I know, I know, he told me. One of the patrolmen saw me and called him."

"Got any burritos, Damien?" Drew asks.

"For you, always," Damien tells him.

"Can I ask what happened?" Damien says.

I turn to Drew.

"Go ahead. You'll tell him anyway as soon as I leave," he says. He's not lying. "But before you start, did the two of you need to tell me something?"

I'm genuinely confused. What haven't I told him that I don't want to have to confess to?

Damien is looking at me like he's worried about whatever I might have done this time that will somehow get both of us in trouble.

"Does Tom know the two of you are purchasing burial plots together? You make such a cute couple after all."

Darn, why does he have to remember everything?

Damien stares at me. "Did you tell him that?"

"No! Ethan ratted us out. Granted, he didn't realize he was ratting us out, but still."

"Drew, I am so sorry. You've been amazing to me and to Tom, and now you're playing a big role in us getting a foster daughter, and I haven't even properly thanked you for that yet." Damien says as he sounds increasingly frustrated and embarrassed.

"Don't worry about it, man. I know how persuasive some people can be," Drew says, tilting his head toward me.

"Still, I'm about to become a dad, and I should know better."

"Seriously, don't worry about it. Just keep me supplied in breakfast food."

"Drew, I promise to make sure our special donuts and any burrito you want are always available to you, whenever and wherever, for the rest of my life. It's the least I can do!"

"Okay, enough groveling," I urge. "Do you want to know what we learned or not?"

"I do!" Aranya shouts from the back.

"So check this out," I start. "Morley sold the mortuary to the Kamfield Corporation before he died."

"But what does that mean for Ethan?"

"He's fired this time for real," I explain.

"Hold on a second, did he even know that?" Aranya asks.

"Yes, he admitted it. The fight he had with Morley on Halloween wasn't one of their usual fights. It was over the fact they had already closed on the deal."

"This may sound like a dumb question maybe, but why was Ethan at work the day we talked to him? Right after Morley died."

I shrug. "I think he kind of hoped if he just kept showing up like he used to, they would keep him on, anyway. But that didn't happen because he was at home today." I turn to Drew. "Can I tell them what you surprised me with when we were questioning Ethan?"

Damien gasps. "You got to question Ethan together like real cops?"

I squeal. "Yes!"

"Oh, cool!" Damien exclaims as he starts to fist bump me, but stops mid-air when Drew glares at us.

"One of us is a real cop. The other one was supposed to just be along for the ride. Scratch that. The other one wasn't even supposed to be out looking for Ethan in the first place."

I roll my eyes and then quickly fist bump Damien anyway.

"The CPPD interviewed the kitchen staff after Morley's murder, and one of them informed us that Ethan did not leave directly after their argument like he told us he did. Instead, he was seen in the kitchen shortly before Morley's murder."

"Nooooo." Damien exclaims.

"It gets better," I laugh.

"Did he admit to poisoning Morley?" he asks hopefully.

"No, he claims he was buying a pot brownie from his friend."

Aranya sticks her head through the serving window. "Really?"

"Really," I nod my head.

"Why is he sneaking around the Hotel Glacier kitchen with pot brownies? Why doesn't he just buy it from one of the shops in town?" Damien asks.

"Do you know how much those cost?" Aranya asks.

"No, and how do *you* know, young lady?" Damien says, slipping back into dad mode. He's getting good at this.

"Pot may be legal here, but it's expensive," Aranya explains. "Or so I've been told," she giggles.

"That's pretty much the same thing Ethan told us."

"It *is* illegal to sell to your friends," Drew points out.

"Here's something interesting," Aranya says as she joins us in the dining area, holding her phone out to us. "Damien already told me that a left-handed person wrote the notes," she explains when I look at her in confusion.

"What am I seeing?" Drew asks.

"Owen Munoz is left-handed," I point out.

"I still don't get it," Drew responds, looking more confused than ever.

"Okay, Mr. I Don't Do Social Media, look at this," I point at Owen's profile where it says he belongs to the "Lefties Are Awesome" group. "He belongs to this group on social media because he's left-handed."

"Oh. Okay. But that's hardly conclusive."

"But it might be a clue!" I plead.

"Might," he emphasizes. "That's a huge might."

"Hey, lady," Marshall says, making a sudden appearance from the back room.

Uh oh.

"I swear, if you've found a body, I really, really don't want to know. Just let it stay there!"

Drew looks askance.

"You want them to find another body in Crested Peaks?"

"Now that you mention it..."

Marcus stomps his foot to show he's annoyed that we're not paying attention to them.

"Okay, what is it?" I ask.

"That guy who said he didn't go to the party on Halloween actually went, but he was in a costume."

"That guy?" I ask.

Marcus rolls his eyes at me. He thinks I'm so dense. "The guy you were just talking about."

"Owen Munoz?"

They look at each other and shake their heads in disbelief, their crooked ears bobbing. For a pair of animals who rely on me to cart them around and feed them most of the time, they sure have an attitude.

I turn to Drew. "The rabbits claim that Munoz was at the party but was wearing a disguise."

"But he told us he wasn't there."

"I get that."

"What kind of disguise? And how do they know this?" Drew asks. For someone who knows how often the rabbits are right - whether he likes it or not - he's still awfully skeptical.

I look down at the rabbits again. "Who told you he was at the party in a costume?"

Marshall starts. "Fufu heard it—"

"Who's Fufu? And what kind of name is that?" I ask, beginning to think Drew's skepticism may be warranted.

"She's a rabbit who lives down the street. She has these itty bitty ears. So weird looking."

"Okay, Fufu told you that Owen Munoz was at the Halloween party in a costume."

"No."

"But you said—"

"You interrupted me." Marcus says.

"Fine. Go on."

"Fufu heard it from Kyle—"

"Who's Kyle?" I can already tell this is going to take forever.

"Kyle is a cat who lives in the alley. Stumpy knows her."

"All right, go on."

"Fufu heard it from Kyle who heard it from Fatty—"

I pinch the bridge of my nose and sigh. "Is there an end to this story? And dare I ask who Fatty is and why does he have such an unfortunate name?"

"Fatty is a squirrel who lives in the park." Marcus blinks up at me like this is the most natural thing in the world. Although to him, I suppose it is.

"I know I'm going to regret this, but why is his name Fatty?"

"Because he's fat." Marshall explains.

I walked right into that one, didn't I? "Are you almost done?"

"Yes," Marcus says. "Fufu heard it from Kyle who heard it from Fatty who heard it from Squeakers that the guy you're talking about was at the party in a costume because he didn't want anyone to know he was there."

"What is taking so long?" Drew asks.

"You really don't want to know," I tell him.

I look down at the rabbits, knowing I'm probably going to regret this, but I have to know. "Who's Squeakers?"

"She's a mouse who lives in the walls at the Hotel Glacier," Marshall explains.

"And she eats like a queen!" Marcus shouts. "You can't believe the food she steals from the kitchen."

Ugh. I'm right, I wish I never asked.

"Do any of these creatures know what kind of costume he was wearing? And just cut to the chase, okay? I don't need to know the entire telephone route."

"Huh?" they ask in unison.

"Never mind, just tell me, do you know what kind of costume he was in?"

I throw my hands in the air at the humans who are all watching us with great interest. If only they knew.

"Ummm," Marshall says as he looks at Marcus, who just shrugs and calls out for Stumpy, who, as usual, comes hobbling as fast as he can whenever the rabbits call him.

"What was that guy wearing at the Halloween Festival? The one who wore a costume so no one would know it was him," Marcus asks.

Stumpy appears to contemplate an answer for several seconds.

"Death?" Marshall says.

"Death? Who dresses up like death? I don't get it. Can you be more specific without running down the list of all your friends?"

Then Stumpy waves his paw in the air, and I don't know why. Is he raising it to say something? Is he waving at someone? I don't know. This is probably pointless. For once, I don't think these three know what they're talking about. The information is like fifth and sixth hand and by the time it got to them it's probably completely messed up.

But then Aranya asks, "This?" as she holds her phone out to them.

"Yes! That's it! Death!" Marshall shouts.

Aranya holds her phone out for me to see. It's a picture of the Grim Reaper.

Chapter 17

"Galloping ghosts, Drew, look at this! I think Munoz killed Morley!"

I grab Aranya's wrist and pull her forward, so Drew can see she showed the boys a picture of the Grim Reaper.

"Are you really going to make me spell this out for you?" Drew asks.

"Who dresses as the Grim Reaper in secret and then lies to the cops about it? Someone who's up to no good, that's who!" I insist.

"Okay, I admit, it seems strange that he would lie to us about something like that. But, we have no proof that he actually lied."

"The rabbits just told you he did!"

"Fufu who heard it from Kyle who heard it from Fatty who heard it from Squeakers told Marshall, Marcus, and Stumpy. Let me just call my captain right now and tell him that, and we'll get an arrest warrant in no time."

"You're welcome!" Marshall says.

"Do you have to remember every little detail?" I complain.

"In my line of work, it helps. And speaking of my line of work, I need to get back to the station. And yes," he says before I can ask again, "I will investigate this further. Meanwhile, if you can find a used Grim Reaper costume lying around, you let me know. Damien, thank you for the breakfast. It was fabulous as always. And you," he says, pointing an accusatory finger at me, "you stay out of trouble. *Please*."

After the door closes behind him, I turn to Aranya. "You heard him. We need to find that costume."

"That's not what he said at all!" Damien protests. "He literally told you to stay out of trouble."

"We need to see if the costume rental shop has a Grim Reaper costume, and did anyone rent it on Halloween?" Aranya says.

"We better pick up Miranda on the way, or she'll be mad we left her out," I add.

"Good thinking!" Aranya exclaims as we head out the door to the sounds of Damien sighing in the background once again.

After we grab Miranda, we head over to the Clever Costume Rentals. One of the best parts about living in a small town is that we can walk almost anywhere we need to go. Thankfully, the store is quiet today. I suppose right after Halloween is a slow time. The clerk at the store is a teenager who's reading a magazine and barely looks up when we come in.

"Hi there!" I wave at him.

He grunts some kind of greeting, nods his head, and then goes back to his magazine. Great, he's going to be helpful.

"Excuse me, can we ask you a question?" Aranya says.

"Costumes require a $50 cash deposit, no exceptions. Rental fees range from $45 to $100 per day depending on the costume. If you pick up a costume on Friday afternoon, you can return it Monday morning for no extra charge," he says in a bored voice while flipping a page on the magazine.

I can already tell Miranda is having none of this. She marches over to the counter, grabs the magazine, flips it shut, and slams her hand on the countertop so hard the teenage clerk isn't the only one who almost jumps out of his skin.

"We have an important question," she tells him. "The least you can do is pay attention!"

"Geez, okay lady, what do you need?"

"Do you recognize this man? Has he rented a costume here recently?" She shoves Aranya's phone in his face with a picture of Owen from his social media account.

The teen looks at her with disdain. "Lady, do you know how many people we've had in here this week for Halloween? I may have seen this guy. I may not have. I have no clue. Now give me my magazine back."

I decide to try a different approach. "Do you keep track of who rents which costume?"

"If they pay with a credit card, it's in the database."

"Perfect!" I rub my hands together. "Can you look to see if you have the name for whoever rented the Grim Reaper costume on Halloween?"

"What's a Grim Reaper?" he sneers.

"Could you please just look it up?" I ask again.

"Fine." he rolls his eyes, stands up, and shuffles over to the computer like it's the most arduous task in the world.

When he asks how to spell Grim Reaper, I have to grab Miranda's arm before she goes to give him a pinch.

As I spell it out, he then examines the screen. "Looks like some dude named Owen Munoz rented it for Halloween."

The three of us stare at each other wide-eyed and excited. My heart hammers so hard I think I might pass out. "We have to tell Drew."

"Whoa, wait, Char, look at this!" Miranda tells me.

"What is it?"

"After you told me that Aranya figured out from Munoz social media profile he was lefthanded, I started combing through it myself. You need to see this."

Under employment, it shows him as retired - he was an exterminator for the federal government where he served on Naval ships in San Diego.

"You're going to have to enlighten me here."

"My Uncle Louie used to do extermination work in warehouses and on the loading docs in San Diego!"

"Erm, I doubt they knew each other? Or did they?" I'm confused as to where she's going with this.

"No, you dummy! It's the poison they use in places like that."

"Ew, I hate to think," I respond.

"They use cyanide!"

"Okay, now we really have to call Drew."

I call him on the way back to Marcall's, thinking he's going to be pleased that I actually called him, instead of just going all rogue and trying to track down Owen myself. He's not. He shouts so loud I have to hold the phone away from my ear.

"Are you telling me that I was barely out the door when you went to the costume rental store after I specifically told you to stay put?"

"Uhhh, well, we picked up Miranda first." The silence on the other line tells me that didn't help. "But this is important, right?"

"That's beside the point, Char, geez. I ask you to stay out of the investigation for your own good, not because I like to hear the sound of my voice lecturing you, believe it or not."

"Okay, I understan—"

"—no, I don't think you do!"

"I have one more thing to tell you."

"Go ahead," he sighs.

Then I explain how Miranda learned he was a retired federal employee, who worked as an exterminator on ships for the Navy, and that they often used cyanide to kill rats on ships.

Another long silence. Is he mad? Did he hang up? "Okay. Send me the link to what Miranda found on social media, and I'll dispatch a patrol car to Clever Costume Rentals for written proof of Owen's costume rental, if, and only if you promise you'll go back to Marcall's right now and stay there. No interviewing anyone else today, understand?"

"Yes!" I respond. "Please, just get the evidence you need that shows Munoz lied to us and then arrest him."

"I'll see what I can do," he says with a click.

I still don't appreciate his skepticism, but I'm somewhat relieved that he's taking this evidence we have on Owen Munoz seriously. He'll come around, eventually.

Chapter 18

Miranda returns to her shop while Aranya and I cross the street to get to Marcall's, and we're caught off guard when we see Neil there talking to Damien. Damien is listening intently and taking notes. Somehow I forgot he wanted him to cater their wedding reception. Turns out Neil is exactly the person I needed to see, anyway.

"Hey guys!" I greet them.

"Hey boss, learn anything new at the costume shop?" Damien asks. "What are you going to tell Drew when he finds out you went there after he told you not to?"

I give him a look that says, not now as I lean my head toward Neil. I know that Shauna and I both got those threatening notes, but I don't think it's a good idea to just talk openly about this until we know for sure. Threat or no threat, I still say Shauna had a reason to kill Morley. Even Shauna admits that!

"Hi Neil, good to see you again! I suppose you're making plans for the reception?"

"Yeah, thanks for giving Damien my message. We're really looking forward to this!"

"When is the big day?" Aranya asks.

"Oh, we already got married!"

"You did? Didn't you just get engaged?" I ask. These two move quickly.

"Technically, yes, but we've known for a long time that we would get married. We just weren't able to do it before now. So we decided it would be easiest just to do it at the courthouse with a couple of friends. This way we can spend whatever we want on the reception and the honeymoon."

"Hey, do you know if Detective Bailey has looked at the security camera footage from the travel agency yet?" I ask. Might as well. He's right here after all. I'm afraid if I ask Drew, he'll just tell me to keep out of it. I need to know which left hander delivered those notes.

Neil shakes his head. "Sadly, the file was corrupted and he said he couldn't get anything from it. Really makes me mad, you know? And scared. I told Shauna she should just close the travel agency for now, until this whole thing blows over. I'm trying to convince her we should just take the honeymoon right away, but I can't seem to coax her away from work."

"Where are you going on your honeymoon? Your bride works in a travel agency; I bet you're going somewhere exotic."

He laughs. "Actually, we're going to Key West. My cousin owns a yacht that we're chartering. We'll visit the islands, go scuba diving, all that good stuff, you know."

"Well, at least it will be warmer there than it is here, right?"

"Exactly."

Aranya and I head into the kitchen and leave Damien to finish his discussion with Neil. I want to ask Drew if he told Shauna that she needed to stay in town until they wrap up the investigation. Maybe he did, but she doesn't want Neil to know she's a suspect and that's why she's postponing the honeymoon.

I may get lectured for even asking, but at least this time I'm not doing anything I'm not supposed to. I'm just here in my cafe, minding my own business. Neil came to see Damien after all, not me.

Me: Hey honey, did the CPPD order Shauna not to leave town until the investigation was complete?

Drew: Are you interviewing her again?

Me: Nope! I'm just here at Marcall's minding my own business and I just wondered.

Drew: Yes, ALL suspects have been asked to stay in town until further notice. See, I told you we're taking this seriously.

So that could explain why Shauna doesn't want to go anywhere, despite the threatening letter she received.

My text notification dings again, and I assume it's Drew telling me to behave.

Hi Charlotte, it's Cody! The gift you ordered is ready!

All right! When we were at the pop-up sale, the other day, I spotted a custom pocket knife at Cody's Chromeworks that I wanted to get for Drew, but obviously I couldn't do that with him standing right there. So I called later and ordered it.

"I need to run a quick errand," I tell Aranya.

I walk into the dining area, but Neil is already gone.

"Everything set for their reception?" I ask Damien.

"I think so," he shrugs. "Now they just need to pick a date and find a place to hold it."

"That's so cool that they want you to cater it for them!"

"Yeah, it will be nice to have some extra money with a kid on the way you know," he laughs.

"That's right, just wait until she wants a car."

"Why must you do that?" he scolds. "I'm anxious enough over this and you go and remind me she'll be driving some day."

"Don't forget dating." I can't help it. He's just too easy. When he tries to throw his pen at me I use magic to send it flying in another direction and laugh. "I'm off to pick up a present; I'll be right back."

"Are you really going out to pick up a present or are you sneaking off to interview another suspect?" he asks.

I hold up my hands. "If you must know, I ordered a customized knife from Cody for Drew for Christmas."

"Oh, how cool!" Damien says. "Tell my cousin I said hello!"

"I will," I tell him on my way out the door. I don't know why he and Drew are always convinced I'm up to something. I rarely am. Only when it's important. Okay, only on days that end in y.

Chapter 19

As I head to Cody's Chromeworks, I start to pass by the travel agency but then pause and glance in the window to see if Shauna is there. While I'm here, I should stop in and ask if she has any updates on the mysterious note writer. No one has to know I talked to her again. And then it hits me. A powerful wave of psychic energy that makes me stumble. I put my hand on the window to steady myself, and the scene from when we first talked to Shauna replays crystal clear in my mind. **I don't care that he's dead. In fact, I'm glad. And I already heard that Chloe, my dad's former employee, poisoned him. Good for her. She should have done it a long time ago. In fact, I wish I had thought of it.**

And then a conversation I had with Drew shortly after Chloe got arrested. **What I'm about to tell you isn't public knowledge. When we searched Chloe's truck, we found an empty syringe. The lab tested it, and it had traces of cyanide in it. The same poison that killed Morley.**

"Oh crap," I mutter, but as I start to turn around, strong arms grab me from behind. "What the—" as everything goes dark, I realize my attacker has stabbed the left side of my neck with something sharp. They say your life flashes before you when you're on your deathbed. But instead of my life flashing before me, I picture Neil knocking the plates off the counter at Marcall's as he was writing the note for Damien because he's lefthanded.

I don't know how much time has passed before I regain consciousness. But I realize I'm not dead, so that's a good thing. But when I try to move, I can't because I'm tied up. My next thought is *idiots*, as I attempt to use witchcraft to untie myself but to no avail. "Hey," I mumble in confusion. Why isn't this working?

"You're not the only witch in town, you know," Neil announces, so suddenly I jump.

"What is wrong with you? Untie me right now!" I demand, as I continuously run through every spell I know that could untie these ropes.

Neil just laughs at me. Why do the bad guys always have that creepy laugh? "You're never going to get those ropes untied yourself. I could tell when I talked to you in your cafe that your witchcraft is only so so."

Jerk. It's one thing for me to criticize my lack of experience. It's entirely another for someone else to make fun of me like this. "What do you want with me?"

"I wrote you a note warning you to keep out of this, but you just ignored it. Even your cop boyfriend told you to stop interfering in police business, but you just couldn't leave it alone, could you?"

"You killed Morley, didn't you?"

"Well, duh. I have to admit, it was rather amusing watching you run around town in a panic trying to track down the killer just so your friend Chloe didn't go down for it. Excuse me sir, I lost my shoes," he says, doing what I consider a very poor imitation of me.

"How long have you been watching me?"

"Ever since you showed up at the travel agency to question Shauna right after Haynes died. I knew that Chloe could easily become a suspect. That's why how we got the idea to plant the syringe on her truck. Actually, considering what a wretched human being that guy was, we could have pointed the finger at just about anybody in town, and people would have believed it. It's just that the enchanted cupcakes, at the Halloween Festival, and flavored with almond extract, gave us the perfect opportunity to not only kill the guy, but solidly blame someone else on top of it."

"We?" I ask. "So it wasn't just you. Shauna was in on it too."

When the door to my right opens, I realize I'm in the back room at the travel agency. The entrance to my left must lead to the alley. I immediately start to formulate a plan to get out that door somehow. I know it's my only hope. They obviously won't let me live after admitting they killed Morley.

"Of course I was in on it," Shauna says, sneaking in the door. I strain to see if anyone is out in the lobby, but my line of sight is limited. I call out for help anyway when Shauna simply crosses her arms and stands in front of me. "Shout out all you want. I locked the front door, so no one is getting in."

I scream "Help!" as loudly as I can one more time on the off chance someone walking by on the sidewalk might hear me. I can be pretty loud when I want.

"What are you going to do with me?" The longer I can keep them talking, the longer I stay alive, and the better my chances are of discovering a way out of here. At some point, somebody will realize I'm missing and come looking for me. Although now I'm afraid they'll look to Owen Munoz and not Shauna and Neil. How's that for irony?

"We obviously can't let you live," Shauna sneers.

"Why did you kill Morley? Aside from the fact you and everybody else hated him."

"My *charming* stepfather was holding back my trust fund. A trust fund that my mother set up for me, and he had no right to take it over."

"Is $200,000 really worth killing over?" I ask.

Shauna barks with laughter. "$200,000? Really? Do you think I'd go to this much trouble for $200,000? Try $2 million, sweetie."

Then she has the nerve to laugh at the shocked look on my face. "Your friend Chloe tell you it was $200,000? Just because she worked at the mortuary doesn't mean she knew everything. If you'd known it was $2 million, you probably would have taken the idea of me as a suspect more seriously, wouldn't you?"

"I thought the trust was set up so you would get it automatically when you turned 28? Why not just wait another year for that kind of money? Why poison your stepdad now?" I ask. This still doesn't make sense.

"So, Chloe obviously didn't know the important details, did she?" Shauna sneers. "Somehow Daddy got the terms changed so if I married a Supernatural, ever, I would automatically forfeit all that money no matter how old I was. And even if I married a Supernatural after I got the money, I had to pay it back."

"You know my parents were about as far from standup citizens as you can get, so believe it or not, I understand where you're coming from. I understand the frustration and anger."

Shauna rolls her eyes at me. "Oh, don't act like you care. I'm not falling for your weird attempts to empathize with me in the hopes that I'll let you go."

I turn to look at Neil. "That's why you just told me you weren't *able* to get married before now. I couldn't understand why you worded it that way. Morley had to be dead in order for you to get married and still get the money."

Shauna rounds on Neil. "What does she mean you just told her that? What were you doing talking to her?"

"I was at her cafe talking to Damien about catering our reception."

"There won't be any reception, you fool!" she cries. "After we dump her body, we have to get out of town! Why do I always have to do the thinking for both of us?"

"You accidentally left the door to Chloe's food truck unlocked after you planted the syringe, didn't you?" I point out. Keeping these two fighting may be what's keeping me alive, and I have a whole lot of ammunition. Pity I just now figured that out, though.

Neil looks at the floor and doesn't say anything, while Shauna shakes her head with disdain. "I can't believe the mistakes you make!"

"Actually, it was your mistake that let me realize you're the one who killed Morley. Although admittedly, I didn't figure it out until it was too late."

"What do you mean, it was my mistake?" Shauna asks.

"When we stopped to talk to you the day after Morley was killed. You said you were glad Chloe poisoned him. But at the time, the CPPD and I were the only ones who knew the exact cause of death. Us and the real killers, obviously."

Shauna glares at me while Neil tries not to laugh at the fact she nearly cost them everything from the very beginning. "Too bad for you then, huh? You could have solved this entire puzzle on day one. And now you'll pay for it."

"I have to know where you got the cyanide." I tell them.

Neil smiles. Who smiles about poisonous chemicals? "You know the cousin in Florida who I just told you about?"

"Where you plan to honeymoon?" I respond.

Shauna groans and slaps her hand against her head. "Is there anything you didn't tell her today?"

Neil glares at her, but continues. "Even though it's illegal, they often use cyanide to catch fish in coral reefs. So, it's pretty easy to get it in Florida if you know the right people."

"You mean the right criminals." I clap back.

"Did you destroy her phone?" she asks Neil.

At the word phone I start to reach for it, out of habit, but then remember that I'm tied up. And that's when I realize it's not in my pocket. I don't know where it is. I must have dropped it on the sidewalk when he knocked me out.

"She didn't have a phone on her," Neil responds.

"Of course, she had a phone on her. Who doesn't have a phone on them all the time these days? My 80-year-old grandmother has a phone and a smartwatch that she uses to order coffee and text her crochet club. She," Shauna points an accusatory finger at me, "had a phone with her, and now it's out there!" She yells at Neil, flinging her hand in the opposite direction pointing to the outside.

If somebody came across the phone and picked it up, somebody else could realize I'm here. "I left my phone at the cafe when I went out. The battery was dead, and I had to recharge it."

"Liar!" she grunts.

"I don't remember seeing a phone," Neil scratches his head.

"You better hope her phone is still lying on the sidewalk where I'm sure she dropped it when you grabbed her idiot!"

Wow, she must be a ton of fun to live with.

The two of them bicker about why she has to nag him all the time as Neil throws open the back door, and Shauna follows him. Intent, no doubt, on proving him wrong once again. I give it everything I've got to get the ropes undone before my only chance at freedom slams shut again, but it's no use. Whatever kind of spell Neil used on these ropes, it's beyond my skills to counter.

But I'm convinced I'm hallucinating from whatever drug Neil gave me to knock me out when right before the door closes, a pair of helicopter-eared orange and white rabbits squeeze inside.

"Marshall! Marcus!" I shout.

"Shhhh!" Marcus warns me. "You want to alert the entire neighborhood?

"Uh, kind of," I tell him.

"Okay, for now, just keep quiet while we work on these ropes," Marshall says.

"Am I dreaming? Is this a hallucination from the drugs they used to knock me out? Are you two really here?"

The two of them give me their customary look that says they secretly think I'm kind of dumb. Being a human and all. And not a more advanced species like enchanted rabbits.

"You take that side. I'll take this one." Marcus tells his brother as he chews on the rope binding my left ankle.

"Oh, you'll never get those off they're mag—. Oh. You did it!" Never underestimate a rabbit's ability to chew through something. What I couldn't get accomplished with magic these two bite through in a matter of seconds. I hold my hands down to let them bite through the rope binding my wrists.

"Let's get out of here!" I tell them.

Thankfully, I think to grab the first thing I see, a fire extinguisher hanging on the wall, just in case we run into the murderous wonder twins on the way out the door. But before I can get to the door, it opens. The look of surprise on their faces when they see I'm free would be hilarious in any other situation.

Neil looks down and sees the rabbits and realizes what they've done. "Why you little—"

When I realize he's about to hex my familiars, I go full on angry mom mode. You want to make a lady madder than you could ever fathom? Try messing with her rabbits. "Don't touch my rabbits!" I bellow, throwing myself between him and the rabbits, blasting him in the face with fire extinguisher foam.

Neil screams and clutches at his face while Marcus and Marshall scurry behind a file cabinet. He was clearly expecting some kind of amateurish spell from me, which he could have easily blocked. What he didn't expect was old-fashioned fire extinguisher chemicals.

Unfortunately, while I'm relishing my victory over Neil, Shauna seizes the opportunity to tackle me, sending the fire extinguisher rolling across the floor. We go down hard as she knocks the wind out of me. I try not to panic as I struggle to catch my breath. It's a horrible feeling, thinking that I can't breathe.

Thankfully, Neil is still clawing at his face and screaming. Not only did it get in his eyes, but he must also have inhaled a mouthful at the same time because now he's on his knees, coughing and gasping for air. Neil is the least of my problems, though, as Shauna takes full advantage of my breathing struggles by trying to strangle me.

I see stars as my head swims, and I realize I'm about to blackout again, when I remember Neil making fun of my lackluster magic skills, and I get mad. I spy a stapler sitting on the desk and focus on moving it. It must be adrenaline because I manage to fling it at Shauna's head, clocking her so hard she falls off of me.

Both of us struggle to get to our feet as I furtively look around the room for another weapon. Both of us scream, however, when Drew and the CPPD burst through both of the doors. It's pure chaos after that as Shauna tries to get away but is tackled by none other than Owen Munoz. How did he get here?

Neil is still on the ground screaming about how I tried to kill him, and they should arrest me. If it were up to me, I'd probably leave him there a little longer, but an officer calls for an ambulance.

After the CPPD secures Neil and Shauna, and ushers them to the waiting cruiser for transport, Shauna shouts back at us. "Ha! The joke is on you guys! We're married and won't testify against each other!"

As the car leaves, Drew rushes over to me. He must be thrilled this has happened again. I've lost track of how many times he's had to do this. "Are you okay?" he asks.

"Yeah, I think so. I'm not sure what they used to knock me out with, though. As I was passing out, I was sure it was cyanide and that I was going to die."

"That's the stuff nightmares are made of," Drew responds softly. "You need to go to the hospital."

"I think I'm okay. Maybe the paramedics could just look me over?"

"Young lady, you need to listen to your boyfriend!" Owen chastises me. "You should see a doctor!"

"Errr, how did you end up in the middle of all of this?" I ask. Just when you think this whole thing can't get any weirder, my number one suspect seems to be riding with the police.

"It's a long and complicated story," Drew tells me. "I'll explain it all on the way to the hospital, but I assure you, Owen is trustworthy."

"Wait!" I grab Drew's arm. "Where are the rabbits? Marshall! Marcus! Where are you?" I'm in full panic mode at this point and feel like I can't breathe again. If anything happened to them, I'd never forgive myself. Meanwhile, Drew looks at me like I must have hit my head when I call for the rabbits.

"Oh, thank goodness!" I cry, dropping to my knees as the two of them squeeze out from behind the file cabinet and race to my side.

"How did rabbits get in here?" Owen asks.

"You wouldn't believe me if I told you!" Drew exclaims.

"You two saved me!" I coo.

"Ahem!" Drew clears his throat.

"You're a big guy with a gun," I point out. "They're just two adorable widdo wabbits wid dere crooked ears," I go on full baby talk mode; I'm so relieved they're okay. I swear I see Marshall stick his tongue out at Drew as they climb all over me and jump around. They're going to milk this one for a long time.

"Hang on a second. How did you two know where I was?"

"We heard you," Marshall explains. I love how they're always so matter of fact when I'm clearly looking for more information than that.

"How did you hear me?"

"We were on our way to the Roses Are Red Flower Shop to see if Beatrice had some pansies for us—"

"—no dude, it was roses." Marcus interrupts.

"Oh yeah, roses. We were on our way to the florist to get roses to snack on."

So much for matter of fact.

"Annnnnd?" I say, waving my hand in a circle.

"Oh, and we heard you hollering for help. The front door was closed, so we ran around back. Then that lady opened the door, so we snuck in." Marshall shrugs as if it was all just that simple.

"Remind me to never complain again about you two running around town begging for treats," I tell them.

"Okay!" they both shout.

I immediately regret telling them that.

Chapter 20

Even though I'm feeling much better, except for a slight headache and some bumps and bruises that will be sore tomorrow, the paramedics insist on taking me to the hospital in an ambulance. And just as they start loading me into the back, I hear Miranda screaming like a banshee.

"Let me go! I'm telling you I need to see her! Charlotte! Charlotte! Are you okay?" I lift my head up to see one of CPPD's finest nearly wrestling with Miranda to keep her behind the yellow tape.

I look at Drew as he groans. "Officer Higgins! It's okay, let her go!"

The officer lets her go with a sigh of relief. I'm sure he wasn't relishing the thought of having to handcuff this wild woman, and then deal with all the paperwork involved with arresting her for disturbing the peace, if he didn't really have to.

Miranda races to my side. "What happened? Are you okay? Holy catastrophe Char, you scared me to death." I try to answer when she smacks Drew on the arm. "What happened here?"

Officer Higgins looks like he's ready to grab Miranda again when Drew signals everything is okay.

"I'm fine," I insist. "To make a long story short, Neil injected me with something, and then tied me up, and then told me he was going to kill me, and then the rabbits freed me, and then I wrestled with Shauna, and then the police came." I take a deep breath. "And now they want me to go to the hospital, for some blood work, to make sure there's no permanent damage from whatever he injected me with."

Miranda stands at my side, staring at me, and for the first time since I've known her, she's speechless.

"Do me a favor and make sure the rabbits get back to Marcall's, okay? After I'm done at the hospital, I'll come back and get them."

Miranda looks over to see Marshall and Marcus waiting patiently by the front door of the travel agency. She turns back to me and opens her mouth, but no words come out. She's still so shocked. I really wish I could get a picture of this. Miranda. Not talking. Will wonders never cease.

□□□□□□

It's late in the evening by the time the doctors release me from the hospital. They wanted to keep me overnight for observation, but I insisted I feel fine and have two rabbits and a cat to tend to. And the cafe won't run itself tomorrow morning.

Although Damien and Aranya would be happy to fill in for me, I'm sure. I just want to get back to the cafe, make sure my friends and familiars are all safe, and let them know I'm fine. They're the best family I've ever had, and I want to be near them right now.

Drew texted them to let everybody know we were on our way back. Miranda bought salads for the rabbits and a piece of chicken for Stumpy, which, according to the rabbits, he said was the coolest thing ever. No one ever just gives him an entire piece of chicken. As long as he doesn't barf it all up in the middle of the night, so I can step in it barefoot in the dark, I suppose it's okay for a special treat.

The adrenalin is wearing off, and I'm already feeling sore. Wrestling on the ground with Shauna took a lot out of me. Neil injected me with benzodiazepine, so while it knocked me out, it wasn't toxic or anything. When we walk in Marcall's, Miranda, Damien, Aranya, Marshall, Marcus, Stumpy, Chloe, and Owen Munoz all swarm around me. Why does Owen Munoz keep appearing in the strangest places is all I can think of.

They insist I sit down while Damien fusses over the red marks on my neck. When I explain it's from Shauna trying to strangle me, he looks like he's ready to run straight to the police station to deliver a little justice himself, all while trash talking Cuban immigrant style. He keeps muttering in Spanish while pacing in a circle punching his palm.

"Damien, it's okay. We arrested her, and we have plenty of evidence to put both of them away for murder and attempted murder," Drew reassures him.

"This is like my worst fear come to life, boss. They could have killed you today!" Damien exclaims.

"It's all good. I swear I'm fine." Who knows how long it will take me to convince him I'm safe now. I'll be paying for this one for a long time. "But while Shauna and Neil were put in the car, she shouted that they won't testify against each other because they're married. That can't keep them from going to jail, can it?" I ask Drew.

He shakes his head convincingly. "We have plenty to put those two away for a long time whether they testify against each other or not.

"I'm still trying to piece all of this together," Aranya says. "Last I knew, we were convinced that Mr. Munoz here," she points at Owen who nods his head at us, "lied to us about not being at the Halloween

Festival but instead he went dressed as the Grim Reaper. Which we confirmed with the costume rental clerk."

"In addition to all the other clues that led us to believe he killed Morley Haynes," Miranda points out.

"Do you want to tell them, or should I?" Drew asks, looking at Owen.

"I can tell them," Owen says. Then he sighs loudly. "As Detective Bailey learned earlier today, I went to the party at the hotel dressed as the Grim Reaper because I planned to confront Haynes. I figured what better day and place to do it, and how great would that have been wearing that particular costume. I wanted to humiliate him the way he humiliated me. But then I realized I would probably get arrested, and even though a tiny part of me thought it would be worth it, I decided against it. And then I went to a meeting hoping it would help cool me down."

"A meeting?" Damien asks.

"I attend a support group for anger management every week. I gave Detective Bailey the name and number of the woman who facilitates it."

"And she confirmed Owen was at the meeting when Morley was killed," Drew chimes in. "She also confirmed, with his permission, of course, that he admitted to renting the costume intending to confront Haynes at the festival."

"Whoa," Aranya whispers.

"From what I was told at the scene," Miranda says, "Drew, Owen, and the rest of the CPPD burst through the doors of the travel agency, rescued Charlotte, and arrested Neil and Shauna. What I don't know is how you got from this," she points at Owen, "to realizing it was Neil and Shauna."

"After Owen's alibi checked out, I circled back with Pete at the Hotel Glacier," Drew says.

"Because he was supposed to be Ethan's alibi," I remind everyone.

"Right, and I still hadn't been able to confirm that. Our friend Pete is very good at dodging my calls," he points out.

"When I told his manager, he told Pete he had to talk to me. But not only did he corroborate Ethan's alibi once he started talking, he wouldn't stop."

"The kind of suspect you like best," I smile.

"Indeed. He told me that Neil approached him before the festival began and asked him if he could switch out a table. Pete would take table number 13, which was Morley's table—"

"Lucky number 13," Aranya mumbles.

"—and Neil would take #17 in exchange."

"That gave Neil the table switching alibi that he originally told me about," I add.

"But at the last second, Neil insisted on serving dessert for table 13. Pete, not wanting to argue with Neil, switched back. After Morley dropped dead, Pete got suspicious—"

"With good reason!" Damien exclaims.

Drew continues. "But when he confronted Neil about it, Neil threatened to turn him into the cops over his illegal pot sales. He convinced him that the penalty was a minimum of 25 years in prison. Pete, not being the brightest guy in the world, believed him and kept quiet. As soon as Pete admitted all this, I realized it was Neil all along and raced toward the travel agency."

"That's where I come in!" Owen boasts as we all turn to look at him. "I stopped at the flower shop, next door to the travel agency, to get a bouquet as I often do, to place on my sweet Maggie's grave. When I came out, I noticed a smartphone in the gutter, so I picked it up. I noticed the cover was the exact same cover that I saw on Charlotte's phone when I was here for a breakfast burrito recently. Just as I pondered what I should do with it, the police showed up! I told Detective Bailey that I found it in the gutter, and of course, he recognized the cover, too. When he ran to the alley, I ran after him."

"You chased the police?" Miranda gasps.

"I got caught up in all the excitement!" Owen slaps his knee. "It was a hoot!"

"I don't know how I'll ever thank you enough, Charlotte," Chloe tells me.

"I kind of accidentally caught the killers, though." I respond, a little embarrassed I didn't solve the mystery earlier.

"You could have been killed, though. All for me. This may sound kind of ridiculous, but you can have free cupcakes for life if you want them. It's the least I could do."

"Your cupcakes are pretty good." I laugh. "It may have been worth it."

"You're out of your mind, but I'm not kidding. Stop by anytime. You don't ever have to stand in line again either."

When Drew realizes how exhausted I am, he starts to herd everyone out of the cafe, promising that they can come back later in the week so we can all swap more stories.

After Owen and Chloe leave, Damien pounces. "What the heck do the rabbits have to do with all this?"

I laugh. "You will not believe this."

"After today, I think I'll believe anything," he says.

"After knocking me out, Neil tied me up with a rope and put a spell on it he knew was too advanced for me to break."

Miranda growls.

"But the rabbits were out looking for pansies—"

"No, it was roses, remember?" Marshall interrupts.

I sigh. These two are incorrigible. "Roses. They were out looking for roses from the florist when they heard me yelling next door. Because Shauna had already locked the front door, they ran around to the back, where I was held hostage. They snuck in the back door and chewed off the ropes."

Damien stares dumbstruck at the rabbits and then back at me. "Did you just make that up?"

"I swear to you that's exactly how it happened."

He shakes his head. "Just when you think you've heard everything."

Chapter 21

The next morning, I insist on coming into work even though Damien and Aranya order me to stay home. What am I going to do at home all day? I'd be bored.

Besides, I would have missed the enormous box that showed in the middle of the morning if I had stayed home. We all stare in disbelief as the delivery man struggles to enter the front door with the brightly wrapped package balanced precariously on a cart.

"Delivery for Damien Torres," he announces.

"What did you order?" I ask.

"I didn't order anything," he responds. "At least nothing that I had gift wrapped and sent here."

"Somebody must like you then."

As soon as I sign for the delivery, Stumpy, Marshall, and Marcus all rush out from the backroom to gawk at the package. "Is that for us?" Marshall asks.

"It's for Damien," I explain.

"It must be for us," Marcus chimes in.

"I just said it's for Damien!"

After the three of them put their heads together, Marshall continues. "Stumpy asks why wouldn't it be for us?"

"Because not everything is for you!" I remind them.

At this, the rabbits giggle. Although when I think about it, given how often they get their way, I suppose it's reasonable to assume presents are always for them, from the rabbits' point of view at least.

Damien and I are still fixated on the enormous package. We're almost afraid to open it.

"It isn't ticking, is it?" Damien asks.

I place my ear against it. "No ticking. But why would you think it would tick?"

"I don't know, something you got yourself into? Some enemy we don't know about yet?"

I rest my hands on my hips and glare at him. "I don't get myself into that many dicey situations."

"Yes, you do!" he declares.

"If it makes you feel any better, I'm done with all of that. I'm sworn to a life of simple cafe ownership. No more crime solving adventures."

Damien makes a noise that I can't quite describe. "Like I haven't heard that before."

"Whatever! Just open the package, would you? Wait, here's a card."

Damien takes forever opening the card. I want to rip it out of his hands and open it myself. He must be one of those people who opens presents very carefully, one piece of tape at a time.

He reads the card and then smiles, passing it to me to read.

To Damien and Tom, Thanks for the burritos. Love, Gladys

"What on earth could this be?" I ask.

"Only one way to find out," he shrugs as he proceeds to open the package exactly as I predicted. One piece of tape at a time.

The rabbits eye him impatiently. I know they're desperate to get their hands on the wrapping paper. Actually, I know they're wishing the same thing I am. That he would hurry and just rip the paper off. Although for different reasons than me. They just like to chew up the paper.

When he finally gets the enormous piece of wrapping paper undone, and drops it to the ground for Marshall and Marcus, they pounce and tear into it while Stumpy sits back and looks confused as to why shredding up wrapping paper is so exciting.

Damien and I gasp when we realize what it is. It's the exact unicorn bed set that they had wanted but wasn't available. "How could she have known?" he asks in wonder.

"Gladys knows everything," I remind him.

"I can't accept this, it's too much!"

"Oh, take it. She's an old woman with no family left. She probably loves the idea of being able to give Poppy this."

"I'll never be late with her burrito again," he breathes.

"How are you going to get this thing home? I guarantee it won't fit in my Prius," I laugh.

"I'll have Tom swing by with the pickup."

"This is gorgeous. How did she find one when you looked all over and couldn't?" I asked.

"I have no idea," Damien responds, scratching his head.

"Never underestimate Gladys' powers!"

As we continue to admire the bright pink bed, Miranda bursts through the door. I need to put a bell around her neck. "You two are never going to believe this!" she shouts. "Guess who's coming to Crested Peaks?"

Damien and I look at each other. "Shemar Moore!" we cheer.

"What? No. But how cool would that be?" Miranda marvels.

"Who's coming to Crested Peaks?" I demand. I swear she's as bad as the rabbits.

"Our fourth favorite reality tv show!" she exclaims, jumping up and down and clapping her hands.

"That's How the Cookie Crumbles?" Damien says.

"Yes!" she shrieks again as we all join her, jumping up and down and clapping our hands. You'd think we hardly get excitement around here otherwise.

"When?" I ask.

"The week of Thanksgiving!"

"That soon? How can they put something together like that so quickly?" I assume it normally takes months at least to put a show together.

"I don't know, but Harvey just told me they're filming it at the Hotel Glacier, and it will be a live Thanksgiving themed pie baking competition with four contestants."

Damien grabs my shoulders. "We have to get tickets, boss. We have to get tickets!"

"How do we get tickets?" I ask Miranda.

"I don't know! Should I go find out?"

"Yes!" Damien and I chorus again, which we really should stop doing.

"Okay!" Miranda throws her hands in the air, spins around, throws open the door and dashes out, declaring, "I need tickets to That's How the Cookie Crumbles!"

"Best week ever!" Damien declares.

"I know!" I agree.

"I mean except the part where you got kidnapped by murderers."

"Of course, of course," I nod my head.

Chapter 22

The big day finally arrives. The day Poppy moves in with Tom and Damien. I insisted Damien take the day off at the very least. Trying to get him to take time off is nearly impossible, but I want him to spend the entire day with Poppy.

I also said if they felt up to it, they should bring her by so we can meet her. I even have some grapes that she can give the rabbits because I thought she might enjoy meeting them. I have warned them that they better be on their best behavior and not get too obnoxious. I don't want her to be afraid of the rabbits or Stumpy.

Damien texts me to let me know they're on their way in and that Poppy is very shy, but she loves hot chocolate with little marshmallows and is excited to meet the rabbits. Aranya and I are standing in the middle of the dining area underneath an enchanted sign I created.

It reads, "Welcome Poppy" with swirling pink and purple colors and a unicorn at the end. After many frustrating misses, I finally discover the proper spell to have bubbles float down from the ceiling to top the whole thing off.

Right before they arrive, we decide perhaps we look a little too eager. We don't want her to think we're pouncing on her just as they get here, so we dash behind the counter and pretend to work.

When Damien, Tom, Bubbles, and Poppy walk in, my heart just melts. Poppy is just a scrap of a thing with pigtails and pink bows. She's nervous at first but as soon as she realizes bubbles are floating from the ceiling she's so busy trying to catch them she forgets why she's nervous. Bubbles, their Pibble, is wearing matching pink bows in her ears and a hat.

"How did Bubbles get a hat?" I laugh.

"That was Poppy's idea," Tom tells me. "She loves her new dog." Damien makes large gestures behind them to emphasize how Poppy really, really loves her new dog. And from the looks that Bubbles is giving her, I'd say the feeling is mutual.

"Poppy, this is Aunt Charlotte, and Aunt Aranya," Damien says.

The poor girl looks like she'll never remember all of that. "You can just call me Char if that's easier," I explain while she smiles. Then she looks at Aranya and says simply, "Yaya." We all laugh, but I guess that's Aranya's new name.

"Marshall, Marcus, Stumpy, come out and meet Poppy."

All three of them come running but skid to a halt the moment they see her.

"You didn't tell me it was a kit," Marshall says.

"I did so. I told you it was a little girl. *And* I told you to be on your best behavior!"

"Here Poppy, would you like to feed the bunnies a grape? They love them."

"Bunnies," she sighs.

I hand her the grapes and she takes them carefully into her little hands. She slowly approaches the rabbits, her hands outstretched.

"You know, if I licked her hand right now, I bet I'd scare the snot out of her," Marcus chuckles.

"You scare her on purpose and I swear there will be no carrots for a week."

"I hear that kits have cooties," Marshall says, eyeing her hand cautiously.

"Oh, you don't even know what germs are, just take the grape."

The rabbits then give me the stink eye as they each gently take a grape from Poppy. She giggles and says, "Cootie."

My mouth drops open in shock as the rabbits turn to me, equally surprised. "Can she hear us?" Marshall asks.

"I don't know." Wow. I'm dumbfounded. Gran and I are the only ones I know of who can communicate with the rabbits. Is it Poppy's age or... Damien has enough to be nervous about right now as a new parent. I don't want him to know what I'm thinking just yet.

"And here's a cookie for Stumpy," I tell her.

She gently hands the cookie to him, but then she tilts her head at him while he tilts his head to match.

"What is happening here?" Marcus asks.

"I still don't know."

"What are they saying?" Damien asks, getting suspicious.

"They're saying they didn't realize she'd be so small."

"Huh. Well, I suppose we should get home now. We've been out shopping for some things."

"More like buying out the entire store!" Tom chastises.

"Oh! Wait!" I tell them. "I have something for you."

Drew and I decided to give Poppy her blanket early. To match her unicorn bed. I'm relieved to see she's a rip open the present as fast as she can kind of girl. It's even funnier to watch Damien cringe as she does.

She squeals with such a high pitch upon seeing the bright unicorn blanket it sends all three of the boys tearing back into the kitchen.

"I think she likes it," Aranya tells me.

"I may never hear again," I answer back.

"What do you—" Damien starts to remind her to thank me.

"Thank you!" she shrieks.

"You're most welcome," I tell her, my ears still ringing.

They carefully bundle her back up to go outside and just as they're walking out the door, Marcus shouts from the back. "When are you going to tell them, the kit is a witch?"

"Not until I have to!" I shout back.

Thank You!

T hank you for reading Cupcakes and Corpses!
Sign up for my email list here
https://mailchi.mp/9ebce0da866a/email-signup-list
Visit my website
biskinnerauthor.com
Follow me on Instagram @bethiskinner Facebook @biskinner-author TikTok @biskinner

Copyright

www.ingramcontent.com/pod-product-compliance
Lightning Source LLC
Chambersburg PA
CBHW031314160726
47993CB00001B/411